A [illegible]le
Further

Tim Oliver

We are the Pilgrims, master; we shall go
Always a little further: it may be
Beyond that last blue mountain barred with snow
Across that angry or that glimmering sea...

Inscription on the SAS Regimental clock tower

ISBN: 978-1-9162473-2-1

1

Egypt, November 16th, 1941

The piercing whine of engines resonated inside the Bristol Bombay transport that bumped down the runway, picking up speed as it fought to leave the ground. Straining against the controls, the pilot peered through the rain spattered cockpit. Inside the spartan interior, eleven men sat, strapped tightly into their seats. They didn't look like ordinary soldiers and they weren't. Many sported beards, all were deeply scored by unrelenting exposure to sun, sand and wind and they had a stillness that only came from enduring and besting hardship. In the dimmest red glow from the shaded jump light, the whites of their eyes showed stark under their steel helmets. Each was loaded down with equipment, from small arms, food, water, maps, blankets and entrenching tools to grenades and specialist demolition equipment. They didn't notice the steel girders that dug into their back and the buffeting of the wind that swirled around them. They had adjusted to just how bitterly cold African nights could be and the weather that day had been worsening by the hour. A soldier spun an unlit cigarette through his fingers, staring into space. Before taking to the air, they'd been told yet again that the success of the operation was dependent on remaining undetected by the enemy. They had trained and toiled to be ready, tuned to a pitch to execute their mission. No one had attempted a night time parachute assault in the desert, and they were relying on the element of surprise to give them an edge. Their targets were the German and Italian airfields at Tmimi and Gazala in Libya. They were to find and destroy enemy aircraft before making their way home through the vast desert spaces. They did not have a sense of it at that particular moment, infused as they were by excitement and trepidation, but they were making history. They were from 'L' Detachment of the Special Air Service, this was their first mission and they were flying toward catastrophe.

The plan rose laboriously into the air, fighting to gain altitude. They were taking off just after dusk, and the blanket of night had fallen swiftly over their group as it made their final pre-flight checks. Captain David Stirling, commanding officer of 'L' Detachment, had stalked amongst the men, a bundle of nervous energy, pausing here and there to exchange a word and a grin with the men. This usually meant stooping down from his 6 feet 6 inches height. A palpable sense of purpose radiated from him as he surveyed the five transport plans being loaded up, parachute containers and men squeezing onboard. This was the culmination of his campaign to gain backing for an elite raiding force who would operate behind enemy lines, sowing havoc and terror in the enemy. It had not been an easy journey. He had battled against an unyielding army bureaucracy that saw his unit as a threat and had himself been derided as unfit for the norms of a British officer. Only weeks before this debut operation, he'd been forced yet again back to Middle East Command in Alexandria to fight for the planes and equipment they needed.

"I'm afraid my hands are tied, old chap," a staff officer drawled. "Alas, your haste was wasted. If I'd known, I'd have let you know so you could have had a shave and bath first." Stirling had gone straight to HQ without changing or washing, and the man's distaste was evident. "There's really not a lot I can do."

"Well, that's simply not true is it? The paperwork I have is in order, and you can do your bit to fulfil the orders of the CIC." Stirling smiled tightly and handed over his orders, signed by the General Claude Auchinleck, Commander-in-Chief of Middle East Command.

The man took the papers and laid them aside without looking at them. "I'm sure it is, but the situation has changed, and your supplies have been reallocated to more strategic needs."

Stirling paused. "You know, the other day someone described the military bureaucracy here in Alexandria as a freemasonry of mediocrity."

The staff officer gaped but Stirling continued blithely. "Layer upon layer of fossilised shit, in fact. Now, of course, not a view I share. A paragon of efficiency, I have no doubt. And one knows all too well that the smooth functioning of the army – and thus ultimate victory - is down to the efforts of supply and organisation."

"Well, quite -"

"And amongst this galaxy of orders, supplies, units and arms, sometimes an order may be mislaid. Entirely natural. But as any staff officer knows, the genius is the person who spots the error and rectifies it. And thus, your opportunity arises."

"Now look here, Stirling, I've heard of your

mob. Running around trying to assassinate people. It's reprehensible and dangerous and I won't be strong armed. We have a chain of command here for a reason. Who is your CO?"

"General Auchinleck." Stirling answered directly to the CIC and that was his weapon in the ongoing war he had been waging against the established staff officer cadre.

"Don't be absurd. I intend to speak with your actual CO at once, and protest."

"Then you will find him just down the corridor I assume? Please, be my guest. Claude is an old family friend."

Stirling bitterly recounted the story later. "You see, the one thing these office types fear above all, is falling foul of someone with more braid on their uniform. Of being disapproved of. Once you understand that, you can work with them." He had gotten his supplies, but again the dead hand of British Army bureaucracy threatened their unit. Many people felt that 'L' Detachment were a stain on British honour, in a theatre of war that prided itself on fighting the 'right' way. Even their name irked some – when asked why they were named 'L' Detachment and not any earlier letter of the alphabet, Stirling would reply with a straight face that it was because they were a 'Learner' organisation. The real reason was to give the impression that a much larger force was operational, but Stirling could never resist tweaking the nose of authority, an authority that had largely damned him and his men. Tonight was the chance to prove he was right, and his idea could work.

"And so, finally, it arrives, Paddy," he said.

Alongside him, a brooding hulk of a man

grunted. Lieutenant Robert "Paddy" Mayne was an ex-Ireland rugby international who drank hard, hit harder and damn the consequences. He had a demon in him that danced when drink was taken and combat joined. On the British Isles Rugby tour to South Africa before the war, after one such drinking spree, he had killed a springbok and left its corpse impaled on the railings outside the South African manager's room. A talented boxer and qualified solicitor, he was just the sort of man Stirling was looking to fill the ranks of his fledgling fighting force. Unorthodox, thoroughly dangerous and a rogue looked down on by the rest of the army.

"It does," Mayne replied. "This weather's no help though."

"No, it's not," the other man with them replied in clipped tone. Lieutenant John "Jock" Lewes frowned slightly as he regarded the weather. He was classically good looking, with fair hair and a carefully maintained moustache, and classically educated at Christ Church, Oxford, where he'd captained the University Boat Club. His early life had been spent in Australia, fashioning a love and respect for the outdoor environment. He was often to be seen frowning, as he was the new unit's Chief Training Officer, responsible for fashioning the volunteers into an effective fighting force, and he was as fastidious in his role as he was in his personality. He didn't, as far as Stirling could make out, have a sense of humour but it suited him. He drove the men – and himself – to extremes, designing dangerous training methods, but always made sure he led by example. The officers in this unit were expected to do all their men did, and more. After a parachute training accident in which two men plummeted to their deaths from several thousand feet, it was he and Stirling who were first to jump the next day. He was absolutely driven and had taken some time to be persuaded to join Stirling, who had a well-earned reputation for louchness and carousing, both qualities Lewes derided, but his brilliance and raiding experience was undoubted. "But we must go ahead anyway. Crusader won't wait for us and this is our chance to prove ourselves."

Mayne nodded. "I know." Operation Crusader was the attack by the British 8th Army planned for two days hence to relieve the German siege of Tobruk. Stirling's force was going to help by hammering the German air defence and bad weather, as intemperate as it was for a parachute jump, wasn't going to delay it.

The men shared a final handshake. "Who Dares Wins," Stirling said, a slight smile on his face. Their motto was freshly agreed and tonight would show how accurate it was.

"I still prefer, 'Strike and Destroy,' Paddy replied. "It is what we're here for, after all."

"Thankfully, you're not in charge." He stuck out a hand. "Best of British. I think it'll be fun."

Inside the cockpit of the lead plane, the pilot peered out, feeling the reverberations of the engines drumming a tattoo on his aching spine. He would not have agreed with Stirling's analysis. The night was utterly dark, and a steady wave of rain was hammering the plane, which yawed sickeningly as it hit a pocket of turbulence. He was thrown sideways, his harness biting painfully into his shoulder. Righting himself, he tried to read the instrument panel, but he could scarcely make out the figures as the aircraft shuddered. Grimly, he fought the controls. The wind had picked up alarmingly after take-off and the Bristol Bombay was pitching and moving with stomach churning regularity as a fully-fledged storm raged around them. They had been briefed that it would take just over two and a half hours before they turned towards the coast, and the plan was to follow flares to the drop zone. Yet in this weather he knew they wouldn't be able to see the flares – he couldn't even make out the coastline, which was their major navigational marker.

"Where the hell are we?" he shouted.

He never heard the reply. Suddenly, the cockpit was flooded with a harsh antiseptic light as searchlights latched onto their plane. The pilot heaved on the controls, trying to escape the long fingers of light, changing direction and altitude. They would escape one searchlight, only to run into the next and the pilot cursed, sweat coursing down his face. The sky around them was lit up by vivid flashes as anti-aircraft guns opened up, and the deep crack of exploding shells sounded ominously close. One shell exploded beneath them, lifting the plane bodily in the air. In the hold, the parachutists shouted in fear, clinging onto their harnesses as the plane bucked. The pilot gritted his teeth – he had to keep on a bearing and speed to allow the parachutists any chance of successfully landing but the flak was all around them and he couldn't shake the lights. He glanced at the speed. Too fast, too fast, they had to slow down. He was turning to his co-pilot when a high explosive shell found them, ripping through the port engine and spreading shrapnel through the craft. Several of the parachutists cried out in pain. They pitched back and forth as the plane dropped, engines dying momentarily before fighting back to life as the fuel flooded in to reignite their momentum. In the cockpit, the pilot scanned the controls, trying to right the plane but he already knew they were mortally struck, feeling the sluggish response and the wind roaring through the holes in the plane.

He turned to his co-pilot but recoiled in shock; the man was slumped forward, and black liquid glinted in the reflection of the instrument panel. He shouted desperately but there was no reply. "Oh Jesus, oh Jesus," he whispered. "We have to turn back!" he shouted, louder this time and with greater certainty, repeating himself. "We have to turn back!"" Feeling a hand on the back of his seat, he sensed the presence of the officer in command of the parachute stick he was carrying.

"We're too badly hit! We have to turn back," he shouted.

"How far to the drop zone?"

"Too far! We won't make it. We have to go back!"

The man grimaced but it was clear they couldn't go on. He already had a number of wounded and they were still under fire. He gave a thumbs up before turning back to the fuselage. The pilot turned back, grimly assessing their situation, making calculations and scanning the instrument panel for speed, altitude and bearing. What he didn't know was that a piece of shrapnel had lodged under the compass, rendering it useless and so, holed, trailing smoke and under fire, the plane began to do a low circle over the coast of Libya.

***

Sergeant James McDuff hit the desert floor with such force that he was knocked momentarily unconscious. Moments earlier, Captain Stirling had dived out of the plane ahead of him. Instinctively, and gratefully after their terrifying journey, McDuff had followed him, immediately seized by gusting wind and driving rain. He plummeted towards earth, swinging wildly from side to side, unable to see a thing until he smacked into the hard desert ground. When he came to, he was being dragged rapidly across the desert floor, his parachute acting as a sail that the ferocious wind was gleefully pulling along, like a dog making off with its owner's leash. In a moment of clarity, he realised it was pain that had brought him round – from smacking into rocks, to skimming over sharp gravel and stones that sliced his overalls and khaki shorts, opening up numerous wounds on his arms, hands and legs. He flailed for the parachute release, finally unclipping himself from the canopy, that flapped joyfully away into the darkness. Around him the wind swirled, whipping up sand that stuck to his face that was soon drenched from the fierce rain.

Rising slowly to his feet, he staggered slightly, checking for serious injury. With relief, he felt he was largely intact, aside from the lacerations and a coating of his own blood. Gazing round in a circle, he began to trudge forward, turning on his torch. He briefly felt an icy clutch of dread that he was alone, abandoned, hundreds of miles behind the front line, but his training asserted itself. One of the reasons he had been selected for 'L' Detachment was his background. The son of a Cumbrian farmer, he had lived and grown up outdoors, hunting, coursing and rounding up cattle in the worst of weathers. He hadn't expected to find similar conditions in the North African desert but, as his old Dad used to say, they were where they were. He was well used to being alone and the SAS training had relentlessly drilled in the need for independence of thought and self-reliance. If the plan went wrong, adapt. If you couldn't meet your objective, find something else to attack. When their fledgling unit had been posted to a desert hell hole called Kabrit for training, they could scarcely muster a working tent or working lorry; promised supplies had been lost, waylaid and otherwise made unavailable to the new unit that was treated with such suspicion by the army. They'd solved the situation by the simple expedient of raiding a nearby New Zealand regiment's camp who were out on exercise, including carrying off a piano.

He'd always found the usual norms of hierarchy and adherence to military doctrine stultifying in the regular army and it had marked him as a man suited to special forces work. Joining the Commando organisation had been a logical step and it was a fertile recruiting ground for Stirling. Yet even then McDuff hadn't seen any of the action he'd craved, as one operation after another was cancelled. And even then, there were one too many rules and regulations and parades and all the manifold irritations of military life. And the heat. After the last raid had been canned, McDuff had gone to stew at a local bar and was sipping his cold comfort when he'd felt a knock behind him from a group of artillery soldiers. "Careful," he growled.

"Or what, matey," the artilleryman replied, swigging from his bottle. He had a beefy, red face and was several inches taller and considerably wider than McDuff. "Take your drink and be quiet."

"Or you and I will have words. Matey." McDuff sank the remainder of his drink and stood up from his bar stool. He felt a keen sense of pleasure at what was about to happen.

"Sun gone to your head is it?"

The barman, sensing the tension, nervously tried to intervene. "Please, sir -"

"Shut it, Abdul," the man barked. "Me and this one are gonna finish our conversation."

McDuff decided that no further words were required. As the man was turning back to him, McDuff's fist, forged and weather worn from the hills of Cumbria, was already travelling. It connected with the man's chin beautifully, and McDuff felt a pure sense of release and satisfaction as the man collapsed. He turned to the rest of the group, letting his anger ride up. "And the rest of you if you want it," he snarled.

The others had backed off but what McDuff didn't know was that, sat in the corner of the bar, was a tall, lanky officer called David Stirling. He had needed some time to think after a meeting in HQ and, never one to miss the chance for a drink, had headed into the nearest bar. There he watched the drama unfolding thoughtfully. Stirling had followed him out of the bar and struck up a conversation. Only later did McDuff realise that he was being gently interrogated but at the time he had become exasperated at Stirling's probing.

"So what is it you want?" he finally said, extinguishing his cigarette with his boot.

"I'm forming a new unit, something like the Commandos but smaller, more precise. The plan is to operate behind enemy lines."

Suddenly, McDuff felt very sober. "Sounds interesting."

"Yes, I rather think it is. So the only question is, do you want to do something special?"

McDuff hadn't needed asking twice and shortly after, he formally joined the Special Air Service. This raid was his and the unit's baptism of fire and he was alone in a desert, his only weapons a revolver and grenades. Not much to take on the might of the Afrika Korps, he reflected but they were where they were.

Trudging forward in the black, he wondered what had become of the rest of the stick. Most of his attention was focused, however, on his surroundings. Many people assumed the desert was a flat featureless plain but it was full of hidden wadis, gullies and shifting dunes, an ever-changing sea, shifting from month to month and year to year according to the vagaries of wind and heat. Sometimes it was just endless sand, others hard rock and gullies. Swampy salt marshes waited to snare the unwary, and hidden dips and escarpments were everywhere. The SAS were trained to not just know this land, but to exploit it against the Axis forces. Yes, they loathed the heat, the incessant sun, the slog that only marching in sand could be. Transporting vehicles was a never-ending round of digging out and toil. For good reason, they'd nicknamed the vast interior 'Devil's Country.' Yet there was opportunity there for those that could make the desert if not an ally, then something to work with.

And so, McDuff was as prepared as he could be for his situation but even so, seeing a flashlight ahead of him was a moment of coursing relief. Stumbling into a half-run, he came across Captain Stirling.

The two men met, and Stirling clapped McDuff on the shoulder. "Good to see you, McDuff," he shouted over the wind.

"You too, sir. Where's everyone else?"

"Scattered. I've found Hancock, but he's not in a good way. Unwin has a broken ankle and Wilson has disappeared."

"What about the equipment?"

"Gone mostly. Come with me, the rest of us are over here."

They trudged over the dune to where the remaining men had gathered. McDuff greeted the other men warmly, but it was clear that the mission was in trouble. And so too, was Sergeant Hancock. He lay shrouded in a blanket, breathing shallowly. They thought he'd broken his back on landing. Alongside him, Unwin lay, grimacing in pain. McDuff gazed down, feeling a sharp stab of horror. Anyone injured would be left behind to make their own way but out in the open desert, unable to move, their chances were slim to none of finding anyone, even the enemy, to take them in. McDuff could see that Unwin knew it, too, and was trying to master his fear, while Hancock at least lay in blessed unconsciousness.

"Rotten luck, Dave," he said, settling down on the ground.

"My Mum always said I was lucky," Unwin replied. "Seems it's run out." He glanced at Hancock before answering McDuff's unasked question. "I can't leave, Reg," he said bleakly. Even if he were able to try and hobble towards a road, he wouldn't countenance abandoning his comrade. "So I'll just have to wait it out. Maybe my luck will come back."

McDuff struggled to find the right words. It was a death sentence. "Bloody weather," he finally said. They were highly trained, physically at their peak and taught to overcome the toughest of environments, yet they were utterly helpless. The men would be left with blankets, water and a revolver. The desert was not conquerable. And there was nothing to be done. ere.

2

Captain Stirling addressed the remnants of his stick. An inventory of men and material revealed the damage the storm and the chaos of the drop had done. Of the eleven men in the stick, one was missing, two were too badly injured to walk, and another two had injuries that negated their ability to participate in combat. Most of the equipment was gone, the canisters disappearing into the desert and they'd spent a fruitless while searching for them. Nevertheless, the fury of the wind had abated, and they felt they had enough men and remaining material to inflict some damage.

"Not a great start, but I am sure we can all agree we must continue."

There were a few nods of agreement, McDuff among them. "Didn't come all this way to turn around, sir," he added.

"Quite. And the fate of our unit may rest on the outcome, so we must make sure we deliver. Sergeant Price will take the walking wounded and make for the rendezvous point. The rest of us will make for the airfield. Hancock and Unwin will stay here. Questions?"

"Any idea how far we are, sir?"

"Hard to say and with celestial navigation out, then we won't know for a while. I think it's safe to say we're not on our dropzone, so we'll head north towards the coast until we find the road." The road was the single highway that ran up and down the coastal strip through North Africa, over sixteen hundred miles from Tunis to Alexandria. It was the road the armies of Africa fought up and down, pinned to the safety of the coast away from the harsh interior and it was on this road that the targets lay; German and Italian airfields spread out like pearls on a necklace, waiting for the SAS, pirates of the desert sea, to plunder.

Trudging away from their stricken comrades, McDuff pushed them from his mind. They all knew that they were really fighting two enemies – the Axis forces and the common enemy, the desert. Yes, they would try and exploit it, to use the fear it engendered to their advantage, but always it was there. Vast, unending, unyielding. Any moment of weakness, any mistake in navigation, was punished mercilessly. The arid expanse brooded, implacable, waiting for you to err, letting the heat and the sand wear you down. Occasionally, it bestirred itself to send a sandstorm to test your defences, to probe and expose any reliance on human technology. When you made an error, when your body gave in, there was nowhere to go, no help to turn to. In the deepest reaches of the desert, death was silent. And when it was over, there was no trace of you left, just the endless expanse of sand that subsumed you. McDuff respected that. It reminded him of the windswept hills of home – it was a hard environment, one that you had to know, one that exposed you if you were weak or arrogant. Being able to work in such a place, to deliver, gave him satisfaction. But whereas before it would have been rescuing a sheep that had fallen down a gulley in a raging northern storm, here it was bringing fear and flame to an enemy who felt safe hundreds of miles behind the front line. And the line between success and death was a sliver.

As so, as he gazed around in the darkness, the usual canopy of stars hidden by the steel belt of dirty cloud that intermittently allowed a weak shaft of moonlight through, McDuff's mind had already moved onto what was next. The pity he felt was already being compartmentalised, rationalised. The men left behind had known when they set off that they would be left if they couldn't move. Just as McDuff knew that he would be, too. Which was why they had been chosen for the SAS. They were physically fit but mentally strong, armoured against the reality that in this harsh, deeply inhospitable environment, the odds were always in the houses' favour, always likely to roll onto black when you had all on red.

He panted as he trudged up another dune, the wet sand clogging his legs, sapping his energy. This was the mind-numbing work of desert warfare and the battle was as much mental. The landscape scarce seemed to shift in front of them, giving the inexperienced the sense they weren't moving forward. It took an effort not to be discouraged and to remain alert, and he was grateful for the brutal training regime that had been imposed on them by Lieutenant Lewes, not least that so much took place at night. In the desert, night was their friend, to hide them from prying eyes, the reconnaissance aircraft of the enemy who would hunt them. Indeed, they had trained during the day blindfolded, just so the other men could study how they moved and behaved without sight. He recalled listening to Captain Stirling and Lieutenant Lewes discussing the expected endurance of a soldier in desert conditions.

"There's only one way to do it," Lewes remarked.

"Which is?"

"I'll do it myself."

Stirling paused. They didn't know what the limits of endurance were for a man in combat. They had markers from civilian trips before the war, but no one had anticipated small groups of men operating in combat conditions behind enemy lines. Lewes' plan was in essence the SAS – barmy, highly dangerous, but in the final reckoning, utterly logical.

"I see. And how do you propose to proceed?"

"Simple, really. I'll walk a hundred paces, which is, what, about eighty odd yards? Then I'll transfer a stone from one pocket to the other. If I do that, all I need to do is keep a tally of the changes, I can see how far I get."

"Well. Best get to it then."

And Lewes did, building up from eleven miles to a hundred, all the while seeing how long it would take him to need to drink, how long it took him before he cracked. Each time, he reduced the water ration he took. Since he assumed – rightly – that he was the near the edge of possible endurance, he would be able to get a clearer view of what the men were expected to do.

Thus began 'Lewes Marches,' vast route marches conducted across the desert. They were conducted in the oven of the day and the ice bath of the night. They were made to practice their navigation, even as the moisture in their eyes evaporated and their spit congealed. McDuff's body still twitched when he thought back to those early days, an instinctive response to the visceral fatigue that wormed its way into body and mind. The stultifying heat and pain that made the siren call of stopping so tempting. At that point, it was no longer a truly physical test, it was a mental one, as they'd been forced onwards, carrying equipment, forbidden to drink their water. For that was what was in Lewes' mind, to build the ultimate discipline - carry the water, but you cannot drink, no matter how arid the mouth had become, how gummed with sand. And you cannot share it either, lest in combat such an act created tension that would be ungovernable. McDuff had felt confident in his physical shape coming into the SAS but Lewes this took his assumptions, mocked them and made him weep for his naivety.

Yet that also built a fierce camaraderie between the men, underpinned by an enduring fear of being returned to unit – of failing the task, of being unable to go on. That fear was so often rooted in underlying personal insecurities and it drove them all on. McDuff had been brought up in a loving but hard environment where praise was sparse and earned, where the minimum expected of him was his obedience and his commitment to the family. He chafed at the constraints but fought to deliver for his father and his younger sister, rarely complaining and if he did, given short shrift by his taciturn father. War was an escape and a chance to be something, to be meaningful and to be exceptional. That was why he was in the SAS, why when Stirling had asked if he wanted to do something 'special' he hadn't hesitated. One private soldier, his boots ruined, walked forty miles through the sand rather than give in. No one wanted to let themselves or others down. Ignominy was being returned to unit – RTU'd. They chafed and they grumbled all the time, but they didn't give in. When they had been digging holes in the sand for four hours on one exercise, McDuff felt he was going to explode with pain, frustration and anger at the seemingly pointless activity – but he mastered himself. And the urgency of their bond was built on the knowledge that the danger they faced, that they overcame together, was real. It was a point of principle for Lewes that training took place without any exterior support. They relied on themselves. If they failed, or went off course, or got injured, no one was on standby to rescue them, no planes would be there to find them.

McDuff looked round as their small group paused. Captain Stirling mentioned them to stay down while he moved ahead. McDuff looked around into the inky landscape. Darker shapes and shadows showed up where an occasional shrub or thorn clung to life. One thing he had learned was to listen, really listen. For the desert was often truly silent. A rustle of wind stirring a sand devil perhaps, or the cry of a desert jay, would lift the veil, but usually there was a powerful, heated silence that lay like a thick blanket over the land. Tonight, it was the turn of the heavens to pierce that with rain and wind, and he wiped away the sticky stand on his face as the party moved out again.

As he rose and took a step, he stumbled on a hidden rock and fell to his knees, cursing. He sprang up, reflecting ruefully that being on his knees had been a regular occurrence since joining the SAS. Not least when they'd learned to parachute, as that had was considered the best means of insertion behind enemy lines. McDuff had assumed that someone from the RAF would be training them, but that notion had quickly been disabused.

"Gather round, gentlemen," Stirling had called, and the men had formed a school circle "Today, we embark on parachute training. An exciting day I am sure you will agree!"

"Can't wait, sir," someone piped up from the back.

"I'm glad to hear it," Stirling smiled. "Now, I'll hand over to Lieutenant Lewes to get us started. Jock?"

Lewes strode to the front. "Thank you. Now, before we begin, I wish to remind you on an old adage that I think will serve us, in this new unit, very well over the forthcoming weeks." He paused, gazing sternly out over the assembled ranks, their faces tanned to a leathery hue. "We acquire more merit on this earth in doing gladly those tasks which are least attractive than by any amount of enjoyable labour."

"Well, doesn't that sound fun," McDuff muttered.

"I actually think he enjoys the pain," Corporal Hanson, who shared a tent with McDuff, replied.

"I think he's a couple of bob short of a pound."

"Today we begin your journey towards full status as a parachutist," Lewes continued. "But before you get anywhere near a plane, we need to ensure you understand the fundamentals of parachuting. Specifically, lateral and vertical movements, while being able to judge speed, altitude and ensuring your safety when you land. Come with me for your first lesson."

McDuff and the others obediently trotted after Lewes, who led them out from the main camp. He came to a halt in front of several battered looking trucks with open backs, manned by grinning orderlies. A pile of what looked like sporting equipment lay on the ground before them.

"Trucks?" Hanson queried.

Before McDuff could reply, Lewes climbed up into the back of one of the trucks.

"Got to be better than another route march," McDuff observed.

"I'd hold fire on that until we see what this is like. This is Lewes after all."

Lewes stood before them, hands on hips. "I'm going to demonstrate the first exercise. This is all about controlling your landing, using your body to go with the force and to avoid injury. It will also get you used to the sensation of falling at speed. To that end, we will be jumping off the back of the trucks to simulate a parachute landing."

McDuff and Hanson shared a look. "Remind me again why we joined this mob?"

"I thought you were bored."

"I was, but now I'm just wondering what the hell the plan is."

"In front of you is some protective equipment," Lewes continued. "Please ensure you have taken what you need."

The men milled around, picking up the bits of gear. "Where the heck is this from?" McDuff asked, holding up a pair of knee protectors.

Striding past, Stirling paused. "Baseball equipment, McDuff."

"Baseball equipment?"

"Indeed. All we've got but I'm reliably informed the Yanks swear by it. Sturdy stuff and should keep you safe enough if you follow the instructions."

"Right you are, sir. Let's hope it works."

Hanson grinned, and strapped on the gear, McDuff reluctantly followed suit.

And so, their parachute training began. First, they watched as Lewes signalled to the driver and the jeep began to pick up speed. Lewes assumed a crouch and then simply rolled forward off the tail, landing in a puff of dust on the desert floor. He immediately sprang to his feet and the driver circled and picked him up again. "That was fifteen miles per hour. So, starting easy. Now we must build. And then you will try."

Once more, Lewes signalled to the driver, who accelerated more purposively this time. Again, Lewes hurled himself off the back, rolling to cushion the impact of the fall, which by the third try looked far more serious. McDuff winced as Lewes hit the deck.

"Piece of cake," Hanson said with a nervous grin.

What followed was a week of the most frightening yet strangely exhilarating training that McDuff could imagine. Lewes got the trucks up to thirty-five miles per hour, and soon the first injuries occurred. It began with sprains and bruises, escalating into broken bones as several men fell hard.

"Perhaps not the most traditional of approaches, Jock?" Stirling asked as another man limped to the infirmary.

"Well, neither is our unit."

"Fair point."

"And this will test their nerve as much as anything. I want to ensure that only those with the highest discipline will serve in the unit."

"Just so long as there are some left at the end."

Lewes frowned. "Are you doubting my methods?"

"Honestly? Yes. But I've come to realise that unorthodox brilliance is what you do best, so carry on."

Mollified, Lewes returned to the fray. The men wandered out one morning to find another test in store. McDuff was among the men examining the contraption when it dawned on him what was in store. "Are you joking," he said out loud as Lewes began to climb a tower. At the top of the tower a long slide began, which ended at a barrier. At the top of the tower was a trolley. Before the disbelieving eyes of the men, Lewes waved and then settled himself in the trolley before pushing off and hurtling down the chute. McDuff found himself holding his breath as the trolley met the barrier, hurling Lewes into the air. "He can't be serious," McDuff said in disbelief, but Lewes once again, miraculously, bounced to his feet and strode over.

"The key is in your position in the trolley," he began enthusiastically. "Legs bent, hands on either side and at impact launch yourself, using the force to catapult forward. Then it's all in the landing. Who's next?"

Eventually jumping out of a plane had seemed easy, despite the accident where two men had died. The feeling of falling, instinctively terrifying, soon became intoxicating; the speed, the view, the sheer joy of free falling, the mild terror that the parachute wouldn't open replaced by blessed relief when it did, allowing you to sway gently to earth. Yet training was nothing like real life, as he had found out jumping into the stormy night and nothing could prevent the desert when it was roused from its slumber, and tonight it hadn't finished with the men of 'L' Detachment.

McDuff doggedly followed Stirling north

towards the coast, their troop down to five men. Dawn had broken revealing a grey sky watching carefully over them. The wind that had tormented them had retreated, and rain spat only intermittently. It felt to McDuff that the desert had itself fallen back, content to see how they would cope as their wounded party trailed through the interior. And perhaps, McDuff would reflect later, he really believed that, but the quickening of interest from the desert came fast and with forceful malevolence. It began with the wind beginning to reassert itself, rousted from its slumber, which prompted its cousin, rain, to return to the sport. The clouds darkened and closed in, and a crash of thunder heralded a deluge that had burst upon them with breathtaking speed, a foaming, writhing mass of water that struck with the force of a brick. They were in a wadi and the rain assailed them, a cold, wet, fat, mass of a million drops that beat them down. Sand became instantly churned to a sludge that coated the legs and made every movement a struggle. "To higher ground!" Stirling shouted, and the men struggled to claw their way up the dune away from the raging torrent, which was rising with frightening speed. Anything not securely fastened was swept away, rucksacks containing their remaining explosives the first to be lost, each man watching in despair as their chance to execute the mission disappeared with them.

McDuff couldn't comprehend being so wet and cold in the middle of the desert expanse, struggling to stay out of the vicious waters that coursed through their position, threatening to drag the unwary away. Behind him came a shout from Hanson as a great patch of sand came away, like an iceberg calving from a glacier. McDuff dived forward, arms outstretched, feeling Hanson's desperate hands sinking into his arms. "Hold on!" he shouted, but for a terrifying moment their momentum continued. McDuff stared into Hanson's face, rivulets of rain running down it, eyes wide in terror, willing himself to stop. He tried to dig into the sand with his feet, but nothing happened, until a heavy weight suddenly fell across the back of his legs.

"Oh, thank god," he said loudly, still not knowing what was trapping them.

"I prefer 'Captain,' came a voice, "but right now, whatever you think is best."

Twisting round, McDuff saw Captain Stirling's panting face and laughed half-heartedly. "Bad time for a swim, Captain."

They regrouped and took stock of the situation as the storm raged around them. "Try the time pencils," Stirling ordered, still hoping to salvage something from the situation.

"Kaput, sir," McDuff said. "Also, the fuses it seems."

Stirling cursed, as did McDuff when he realised that his cigarettes were another casualty. "Bloody weather," he muttered, trying to shift into a more comfortable position. "This is hopeless," he added to Hanson.

"Yeah," Hanson replied morosely.

"All this way for nothing. And Reg and Derek and Barry, all gone."

Hanson didn't reply. There was nothing to be done and nothing to be said. They watched as Stirling stalked out into the desert, hands on hips and gazing into the bleakness. A dirty, grey visage expanded before him. The rain pounded unceasingly, dripping from his face unnoticed. The culmination of his campaign had come to this. A force crippled by weather and accident before even catching sight of an enemy. His plans were in ruins. The desert mocked his ambition.

"Orders, sir?" McDuff asked.

"Home, McDuff. We go home."

It was a near forty-mile march to the desert rendezvous and for McDuff, even after all the Lewes marches, the incessant training, the physical and mental degradation of the preceding months, it was the hardest time. The weather at least gave them respite from the preying eyes of enemy reconnaissance, but their steps were dogged by the knowledge of their failure. It was the worse kind of failure. To not even locate their target, to not even contact the enemy and still to lose men and materials; lives had been lost for naught. And the scale of the defeat only became apparent when they contacted their transport, the men of the Long Range Desert Group, who waited in the desert reaches to ferry them home. "Over here, Pommies," came a voice out of the gloom in the distinct twang of New Zealand. The piratical men of the LRDG appeared, wearing a rag tag of keffiyehs, caps and bits of uniform that was only used if they helped the team in the desert. They were reconnaissance specialists, roaming the desert to spy on the enemy and providing the vital intelligence for the Allies. Their trucks encircled a small fire hidden in a shallow hollow. One of them offered McDuff a steaming tin.

"Bully beef never tasted better," he said gratefully.

"That's because it's laced with rum."

They brewed up and waited to see who else would return. As the time ticked by, Stirling became ever more agitated, spending time starting out into the desert as if to will the remaining members of his force to appear. Paddy Mayne made it back, along with Jock Lewes and a few of his stick, but it was clear the mission had gone horribly wrong from just how many men hadn't made it back to the rendezvous.

"We need to get going, Captain," the commander of the LRDG group finally suggested to Stirling, who stiffened in instinctive refusal, before the tension went out of his shoulders. He sighed.

"Yes, we should." He gave one last look around before turning. "Let's go home."

And so the remnants of the SAS's first mission set off. They were glum as they bounced along the uneven desert road, leaving behind dead and missing comrades.

"What a bloody mess," McDuff said.

"Yep. I joined this lot to stick it to Jerry, not attempt suicide by parachuting into a storm."

"I really thought this was going to be different. All we did in the Commandos was have cancelled raid after cancelled raid. Barely saw the bloody Germans. And now this. Christ." McDuff stared into the desert, wondering if he'd made a terrible mistake. "I mean, the lads are fantastic, but it can't work like this. There's no point being shot out of the sky before you reach the target, never mind jumping in a storm. It has to change."

"How else are we going to get there?"

"Well, what about this lot?" McDuff gestured around them. "They've gotten us out, why can't they get us in?"

"Because transporting sixty odd men across hundreds of miles of open desert towards the enemy is very different from getting out."

"Bollocks to that. It's this or the whole bloody lot of us may as well be RTU'd."

"Agreed," opined one of the men from Mayne's stick. "We actually reached the airfield so if we can get in then we could do some damage." Mayne had his men had had the frustration of no working explosives and an open attack with grenades would have been suicide.

"Yeah, maybe it could work," McDuff said thoughtfully. "It better. Because I didn't join up to do nothing." He thought back to his interview with Stirling. Instinctively, he'd felt this was the right fit for him. Away from endless drills and parades and spit and polish. Away from overbearing officers who barely knew their arse from their elbow. Away from an army that still seemed to be treating the war as some kind of 19th century colonial squabble. Stirling offered freedom from all that, a new way of waging war and not just that but an effective one. McDuff grimaced. It had to work.

In the lead jeep, Stirling, too, was thinking of the future. They faced a fight when they returned, he was sure of it. If they could get home, they could regroup, they could rebuild and try again. But only if they were allowed to, only if the bureaucracy and high command that largely hated them could be persuaded that this disaster didn't mean that the Special Air Service would be still born. here.

3

Emily Daws pushed her glasses back, simultaneously tucking a loose lock of sandy blonde hair behind her ear. It was an impatient gesture and for those who knew who, signalled her intense irritation. Leaning over the desk, Major Rossi followed up his clumsy invitation, hopeful and naïve, blithely unaware of the real feelings he was eliciting.

"As I said, I feel we have much in common, and could be good for each other." He smiled unctuously, a waft of stale gin as unpleasant as his words reaching her.

Unpleasant? Perhaps tedious, Emily reflected. She had no illusions she was a beauty queen but knew that many weak men had found in the heady days of war an opportunity to sleep with more women. It ever thus, she thought. A war on and if felt as if many men thought it was a great chance to have a shag. It had been the same in London and it was the same in Africa. The fact that it had been Englishmen then and Italians now really made no great difference. Although with the minor detail that if Major Rossi knew who she really was, she'd be taken outside and shot.

She forced a compliant smile. "Major, you are incorrigible. But I don't think it all appropriate while my fiancé is fighting the British as we speak." Her imaginary consort was flying in the desert skies with the Regia Aeronautica and, thus, conveniently absent.

"And as a proud Italian, he would no doubt applaud my intentions! Beautiful women are there to be admired, Senorita Agosto."

She chuckled coquettishly, she hoped, wondering yet again at the inherent optimism of the opposite sex. Some of whom, she reflected, were sometimes quite simple to manipulate. "Between you and Colonel Ferroni, I am sure he is as concerned for my virtue as he is the British fighters!"

Major Rossi frowned. Colonel Ferroni was his sworn enemy. It was a personal and professional vendetta. Ferroni had much of what Rossi lacked and craved for himself, notably good looks and connections in Rome. Rossi also served in the Servizio Informazione Militari, the Italian Military Intelligence service, while Ferroni was a member of the OVRA, the Italian political police that patrolled anti-fascist sentiment in Italy. Rossi considered himself the purer fascist and had always doubted Ferroni's loyalty, despite his position with OVRA. "I would be very careful of the Colonel," he said sternly. "That man does not have the interests of the nation in his heart, only himself."

"Of course, Major." Major Rossi may be a fool, she reflected, but what he knew, she needed to know.

As Major Rossi leered at her, she thought back to just over a year ago and how radically her world had shifted. Her previous self would have found this an impossible situation to imagine. And if she were honest, she still did. She'd been working as a secretary in the Secretary of Supply, which was stultifying, although she felt she was at least doing her bit. Yet life in London was exciting – the bars were full, the music halls packed and a defiant spirit of seizing the moment pulsed through the capital. Even as the German army rampaged across Europe and the bombs had started to fall, a cheerful stoicism seemed to infuse the city. It was frightening, liberating and intensely real in a way that life before had never been. She, like millions of others, had gone from monochrome to bright colour in weeks, and while some were unable to cope, she was invigorated. Yet in that invigoration were seeds of impatience, of the feeling that there was more to do. But she was unsure how that was going to happen, and so had fallen into the London life, as carefree as they could make it, enjoying the music, the atmosphere, shrugging off the indignities of rationing and the tedious propaganda and finding escape in the bars.

It was in one such bar that she'd met Peter. As she waited to be served, barely able to see the far end of the room through the fug of tobacco smoke, a slight nudge at her elbow made her shift position. A glance to her left revealed a uniform and she thought nothing of it. You couldn't swing a cat without hitting someone in uniform, from every conceivable nation across Europe. London had become the melting point of Europe, crowded with nationalities and people from all walks of life. She'd once found herself at Tottenham Court Road tube station during an air raid next to a man in a dinner jacket with impeccably groomed pencil moustache, who'd politely shared his dinner with her.

Over the noise, a voice sounded loud in her ear. "Perhaps I can buy you a drink?" The voice was heavily accented, and the offer instinctively irritated her. She'd been at her desk for hours that day, typing, typing and more typing. Her back was sore from hunching over and her calves needed a proper stretch. She hadn't felt like going out for once but been corralled into it by her friend, Mavis. What she wanted was a couple of drinks, maybe have a dance and then go home.

"No, thank you," she said coolly, though on seeing the earnest face, she softened her refusal with a small smile. He was so young, she thought, though she herself was only twenty-six.

"But you so lovely," the airman tried, smiling. Emily noted the Czech flag on his shoulder, explaining the man's broken English.

"That's as maybe, but I'm afraid I am just after a quiet night tonight." She smiled again and turned away. Yet almost immediately, a tap came to her shoulder.

"I am leaving UK tomorrow, very dangerous for me. This is my last night!"

Emily's patience, already thinner than usual, snapped at this point. The line was so well worn, her refusal placid, that this further intrusion infuriated her. "Why don't you just sling yer hook," she scorned, settling instinctively on a phrase she'd heard being bandied around by Mavis.

"I'm sorry, my English is not so good. What does this mean?"

Emily rolled her eyes. "Try this then." And without planning to, she told him to piss off in long, poetic and completely fluent Italian.

There was a brief silence as the airman looked at her in confusion. The third language had not clarified the situation, although Emily's tone had given him a clue. As he began to speak, a hand closed on his arm and the man the other side of him, offering her a disarming smile, spoke quietly into his ear. The airman looked at the man, back at Emily, before muttering an oath, cramming his cap back on and disappearing into the fug.

Emily turned warily to her putative rescuer. Not that she in any way felt she had needed rescuing and was thus deeply suspicious of the man who gave her a small smile. She examined him. He was shabby. That was the only word. Dandruff on the collar of his trench coat, a battered trilby in his hands. Poorly trimmed nails, she noted. His trousers felt a touch too long and his shirt just a touch out of fashion. His face was more interesting. An open face, guileless at first glance, but there was a strength there, a look of someone who was comfortable with himself.

The man extended a hand. "I'm Peter. And please let me assure you I have no interest in trying to buy you a drink."

"Good. I can take care of myself quite well, thank you."

"I don't doubt it. I just wanted to get rid of him as he was blocking my way to the bar."

She smiled despite herself. "So, what did you tell him?"

"I told him you were a prostitute, I was your pimp and if he didn't move on, I'd send back to Prague in a box."

For a moment, she stared, then threw back her head and laughed. "Really?"

"Really. These young chaps like to think they're all daredevils and all that, but most are remarkably conservative at the end of the day. Especially the Catholics. All that guilt, you see."

"And what you know about guilt?"

"Nothing. I am but a brutish Protestant, and helpfully for me, guilt isn't that useful for what I do."

"And what it is you do?"

"I was going to ask you the same. I couldn't help but notice you spoke Italian just now?"

"I did and you haven't answered my question."

"I know but I'd still like to know why you speak Italian so well. Tell me and I'll tell you my job."

"Fine. If you must know, it's in the family. What else."

"And you speak it fluently?"

"Why?"

"I'm a curious sort."

"And overly familiar. But yes, I do." Of all the conversations she had been subject to in bars in London over the previous months, this was the most curious.

"What do you do now?"

"You first."

"Fair enough. I work for the Inter-Services Liaison Department."

"That sounds as thrilling as my work. I work for the Ministry of Supply. What does your department do then?"

"Oh, we help the services work together more effectively. Like the oil in a machine. A humble role but one of increasing importance, I flatter myself to think."

Very general and entirely ordinary, Emily noted. She felt a small shiver of interest, however. There was very clearly something more to this man and his work than he was prepared to admit. "And does finding civilians who speak Italian enter your remit?"

"Well, funnily enough, we've just had an opening for an Italian speaker."

"That seems almost comically unlikely. The Italians are not on our side if I remember correctly."

Peter smiled. "Very true. But there are many Italians who reject Mussolini and his fascists. Many of whom are willing to help us. Alas, finding Italian speakers can be tricky."

"And what would this work involve then?" Emily took a sip of her rum and lime. Her last question had been instinctive; she wanted to know more, and the aura of a hidden story behind Peter intrigued her.

"Well, may I suggest you call on my office on the Strand? We can discuss in detail and you can meet my boss, Mr Griffin."

He'd left her his card and thus began her journey to North Africa. The courtship was brief and efficient. Nothing was hidden from her, none of the perils not made clear. The proposition was simple. To take a role within the Italian military establishment and report back vital intelligence. Her inevitable questions were answered smoothly, her doubts allayed speedily. A fictional Angelina Agosto had already been created, a back story invented and painstakingly set up. The Italian military was constantly seeking secretarial support in its overseas headquarters, made harder by the regime's insistence that women were there primarily to create sons and soldiers. An application would be made, at the appropriate time, correspondence entered into and a date fixed for the arrival in Libya. The shell needed to be animated and was waiting for the right person to step into her shoes. Emily was that person. The only relevant factor for her was how much she was willing to risk. In the final analysis, as she sat in a windowless office in front of Peter and Mr Griffin – an urbane, charming man who had a ruthlessness that made Emily shiver – her reply to the final question was as instinctive as her desire to find out more had been from Peter. "Yes, of course I'll do it," she replied firmly.

Covert training had been intensive, thrilling and intensely frightening. How to correspond with base, how to use a radio without being detected by enemy units, how to disable someone in unarmed combat; all essential skills required of the successful agent. To her mild surprise, she took to it immediately. She realised that, to an extent, her whole life had been playing a part. The dutiful daughter to her widowed mother; the prospective wife to the appropriate suitors she was gently steered towards; the efficient secretary who did what was asked with minimal fuss. Taking on Angelina was another role yet far more thrilling, full of vivid colour. Crucially, she had an uncanny ability to memorise information. As a child, her father had forced her to learn the classic poems of English literature. What started as a burden became a treasured memory of spending time with him before his death from the residual effects of poison gas from World War I. It now served to equip her in her new role, one she embraced more each day. The idea of being caught and shot didn't, truly, occur to her. And so she trained hard, becoming fitter than ever, forced to learn her part until she became more Angelina than Emily.

Despite that, the early days in Benghazi were absolutely terrifying. Her posting was to the headquarters of the Italian XX Corps, the Corpo d'Armata di Manovra, an armoured force that contained the famous Ariete and Trieste divisions. The city had surprised her – it felt decidedly European, with Italian faces everywhere, a legacy of thirty years of occupation and the importation of thousands of Italian colonists. There was even a famous local beer, Cirene, which was exported back to Italy in droves. She had settled in the Italian Quarter along with most of the other HQ staff. Strolling towards headquarters down the wide Via Briccola with its high, white buildings, or promenading through the cooler colonnades to buy a trinket or a date, one could almost forget it was Africa. The tricolour was ubiquitous, the red and white cross of Savola emblazoned in the middle, and it fluttered gaily across the major streets and plazas. Perhaps the most strikingly immediate impact was the heat, ferocious to her sensibility during the rainless and humid summer months after her arrival in June 1941. Not long before, the Allies had taken control of the city in the endless back and forth tennis style combat that characterised the desert campaign, but Benghazi felt solidly Italian and were it not for her occasional touchpoints with Alexandria, she could have been lulled into the life there. Sauntering down the Lungomare, the wide promenade by the sea, sipping a beer in one of the little cafes and everywhere the smiling, relaxed face of the enemy. It was hard sometimes to believe that she was part of a battle against a vicious fascist regime. Her cover, at first seemingly so shabby and certain to lead to her doom, had been taken unquestioningly and so, in the early days, she simply kept her head down and established her life there, exactly as Peter ordered. She wasn't to attempt anything until her first check in where should receive further instructions. So, she took notes, she made friends, and settled into a routine. At times, she almost forgot she was a spy, but even after the terror of establishing contact with Alexandria, time went slowly. She was told to her stand her ground, continue to build relationships and if possible, get close to the

Italian intelligence organisation.

Which had led her to a job working for Major Rossi. It had happened, as so often in these cases, quite by chance, as she gossiped with a colleague over lunch. Rossi was a known lecher and had found staffing his office increasingly difficult after a scandal involving a previous secretary.

"No one wants to work there, and anytime someone is assigned they pull every string in the book to get out of his office."

"I'm not surprised, he sounds awful," Emily said, on alert.

"They're even offering extra pay now, as it's more classified work." Her friend laughed. "More like danger money. I daresay the only classified files Rossi wants you to look at are in his trousers."

Emily giggled. "To be honest, I could do with the extra money. Things are tight at home."

"Really? You'd risk the odious Major Rossi for a few more lira?

"I can handle him. And I need the cash. How can I make this happen?"

"Honestly? Your best bet is probably to stumble across him at lunch and flirt with him. But I know the secretarial pool supervisor, so I can put in a word if you like?"

"You're a star," Emily said warmly. "Thank you."

"You won't thank me when Major Rossi has had his afternoon gin."

Emily laughed but was thrilled and excited and scared all at once. Would she survive the enhanced security vetting? What would she need to do? But it was only once she had received her instructions from

Alexandria that she felt truly afraid. They had a job for her, it was urgent, and she would have to risk it all to succeed.

***

"You left with sixty-five men. You returned with twenty-two. You failed to inflict a single casualty on the enemy or, indeed, on any of his materiel. Not quite what we were promised was it?"

McDuff winced, glancing at Captain Stirling, who sat straight backed on a chair before the military panel arrayed behind of a wide desk. The day after their return to the Siwa Oasis, he had been summoned to Stirling's tent. Paddy Mayne and Jock Lewes were lounging, and judging by their countenances, a difficult conversation had been taking place.

"I need to go to Alexandria, McDuff," Stirling began without preamble. "Can you drive?"

"Yes, sir."

"Good, then you're driving me. We leave at 0600 tomorrow. Questions?"

McDuff had several, but felt it was wise to contain them. "None, sir."

They'd set out as the sun was rising, revealing the sterile beauty of the desert. The burgeoning light was shot through with pink and orange hues, splashed against an icy blue background. As they bumped along, the only sound the engine gunning as it fought for traction, a lump formed in McDuff's throat. He gazed into the expanse, the outlines of sand-blown rocky outcrops emerging, passing tenacious shrubs that sheltered wary rodents and an occasional cluster of hardy acacias. The air was still crisp at this time and the silence peculiarly oppressive. He still wasn't used to the feeling of irrelevance that the desert engendered, that feeling of insignificance. And it made him think of the men they'd left behind, of those that had died out there, alone. He wondered what it had been like. How long did they last? Did they find a peace as they looked up into the night sky, where the stars were so crisp and bright, you felt you could reach out a hand and pluck them? How would he feel in the same situation?

"Beautiful isn't it." Stirling, sat in the passenger seat, disturbed his reveries, gesturing around.

"Truly," McDuff replied with feeling. "And so deadly."

"Aye. Like so much of life. But we can make this world work for us, McDuff, I'm absolutely sure of it. The enemy sees arid waste, impassable tracts of land, the Great Sand Sea. And that's just the British army." He laughed, a tinge of bitterness. "We just have to make sure they don't stop us."

"Do you think they will?"

"One would hope not, but we're about to find out. You'll come in with me, I want as many of us as possible to understand this, and what we must do to make it work."

As the sun rose, McDuff shrugged off the greatcoat that was necessary in the chill of a desert morning and they continued their journey, both lost in their own thoughts. An occasional gazelle was startled out of tis hiding place, and McDuff kept a wary eye on the sky, but they eventually arrived in Alexandria. It was impossibly, overwhelmingly hectic after months in the desert. The buffeting of noise, the chatter, the smells of spice, of dung, of petrol, the vivid colours of market stalls patrolled by their frenetic traders, offset by the drab olive of the multitude of military vehicles scattered everywhere, made his head swim. A stray camel bared its teeth as they squeezed past towards their billet, where McDuff gratefully settled, lying back and watching the ceiling fan gently stir the hot air from one side of the room to the other.

They'd not had long to wait before their summons to HQ, an austere building hidden behind waves of sandbags. The sentry had saluted them smartly as they'd entered, before they'd ascended to the conference room where they now sat, or in McDuff's case, stood at the back. McDuff noted a slight stiffening of Stirling's back when the question was posed to him about the SAS's lack of success but otherwise, he seemed unperturbed.

"Not a bit, but the conditions were exceptional," he replied firmly, "There hasn't been a storm like that in thirty years."

"Which rather beggars the question, why did you jump?"

"We couldn't turn around then, sir. And it wasn't just the jump, it was the flash floods once we were down as well. Despite this, and in the face of incredible challenges, two of our parties still managed to reach either the airfield or the coastal road undetected. Think on that. The men are right, if we can get them there. And of those that did make it to the rendezvous, all were successfully evacuated."

"But will it be so simple next time?" one of the senior men demurred, sliding a paper toward Stirling. "Intelligence intercepts from the Fliegerfuehrer Afrika, no less, show that the Germans are aware that a sabotage operation with five planes was mounted, with targets being most likely airfields. One of our agents has also corroborated this."

McDuff fought to keep a straight face at this news. It could only mean one of the captured men had talked – or been forced to talk. And it meant the enemy would be on high alert for them.

"We were never going to do this just once, so at some point the enemy would be aware," Stirling replied. "It doesn't change the essential viability of the project, gentlemen. We can make this work. We need to continue. Not least as next time we will be using a desert insertion to remove the element of the weather."

"This is using the men of the Long Range Desert Group?"

"Correct, sir. They got us out safely and they are a first rate force for reconnaissance, but not combat. If they can get my men close, we can do the rest."

"Kill the enemy?"

"And their planes, sir. It's what we are here to do."

"Evidently with rather mixed results thus far." The general shuffled some papers. "The LRDG. Would they agree with your analysis of their skills?"

"Yes, sir. I've already discussed it with them, and they'd be quite happy to help. A sort of desert taxi service, if you will."

A silence hung briefly over the room at Stirling's meagre sally. "Taxi service," one muttered, shaking his head. McDuff felt a trickle of sweat run down his back as the panel conferred in hushed tones. Stirling glanced back at him, raising an eyebrow. So much rested on this, not just for the unit but for him, personally. It was agonising having his fate resting in the hands of men who simply didn't understand what they were trying to do. Nonetheless, he was intrigued as to why they hadn't already been given the news that 'L' Detachment was to be disbanded. Why the questions on future operations? Why the discussion of the LRDG?

The general leading the panel cleared his throat. "Against my better judgement, it has been decided that you are to be given one more chance. Your force is highly irregular, Stirling, and to my mind has already demonstrated a lack of the core values of the British Army, not least in the outcome of your first mission. Nonetheless, the overall strategic situation remains perilous and, for now, the fate of a handful of men is not high on the CIC priority list. We also have some work for you to do, which I'll let Major Morris brief you."

The briefing broke up, and McDuff stood rigidly to attention as the assembled brass marched out. He reflected how little he missed all of that nonsense now he was with 'L' Detachment. When they did so, he turned to Stirling with a delighted grin, forgetting momentarily the presence of another senior office in their midst.

"Fantastic, sir, we're still on!"

Stirling smiled back. "That we are, McDuff, that we are. But perhaps we should wait for our conversation with Major Morris before popping the champagne corks?"

McDuff coloured and nodded, dipping his head to Major Morris who approached them. Morris was the adjutant to General Ritchie, the newly appointed commander of the Eight Army, who was one of Stirling's few supporters in the high command. He held out a hand to Stirling. "Good to see you,

David. And I take it this is one of your rag tag army then?"

"Yes, sir, this is Sergeant McDuff. He was on the raid and made it to the coastal road with me."

"Capital. Well, Sergeant, how was it?"

McDuff started, not expecting to be brought into the conversation. He marshalled his thoughts. "It was just the weather, sir. If we can get there, I think we can do it."

"Couldn't have put it better myself," Stirling said. "And, look, I know this isn't what we had in mind, but I'm convinced it will work."

"I dare say, you're right, although many would disagree. However, the situation is that the army's bad luck is your gain – or to put it another way, HQ have bigger things to worry about than your private army. Come, let's sit."

Stirling and Morris sat, but McDuff remained standing, until Stirling waved him over. "Come on, McDuff, have a seat." Morris raised an eyebrow but acquiesced.

"I take it the offensive isn't going as planned?"

"The Auk isn't happy, which is why General Ritchie has been put in charge of the 8th Army. Rommel has caused some chaos. In broad strokes, Operation Crusader had two prongs. The first was for XIII Corps to cross the border into Libya, to contain and capture the enemy garrison towns on the coast, before turning and heading west towards Tobruk. Meanwhile, to the south, our armour is concentrated in XXX Corps, whose job is to head around the enemy positions, to engage and destroy and destroy the enemy armour, before turning north west towards Tobruk."

"Sounds sensible enough."

"Yes and no. But then, when do operations ever go to plan? XXX Corps have had some success cleaning up the coastal garrisons and there have been several confused armoured engagements around the Tobruk perimeter and further inland. But the attrition rate, especially on our armoured brigades has been heavy."

"I'd hate to be a in a tank, sir," McDuff observed.

"It isn't pretty and the chaps we're up against - 21st and 15th Panzer from the Jerries, supported by the Italian Ariete and Trieste armoured divs – know their onions."

"And they're commanded by one of the best," Stirling put in.

"Quite. Which is what is causing us our current discomfort. Seems Rommel has decided to go for the jugular. He's pushed his armour east in a dash towards the rear, and once their armour is loose there, they can cause chaos. And we risk them cutting off our forces between the border and Tobruk."

"What's the current situation?"

"A bugger's muddle. But as you know the desert war is as much a war of supply as anything else. And so, the further east he goes, the more stretched Rommel's supplies are. And the more he fights, the more tanks he loses. He has to either end the battle quickly or capture our supply dumps."

"Surely, the best defence against this is attacking him in his rear?"

"Trust you to reach for that, David, and yes, it is. We need the garrison to link up with XIII Corps and we need to continue to wear down his forces around Tobruk. Rommel is going to have to start fighting his way back west soon enough, as long as we can contain him."

McDuff noted that Stirling had become even more alert at the last exchange. Vulnerable supply lines gave the kind of opportunity the SAS were designed to plunder. "And while you contain him, we can do some damage," he said wolfishly.

"We certainly hope so, or at least an improved performance."

Stirling stiffened, but accepted the point. "There won't be any mistakes this time."

"I should hope not. I'm not certain that another failure can be countenanced, David, so make sure. Now, your fortune is that in support of Crusader, a mixed force under Brigadier Reid from 29 Indian Brigade, set off to capture Jalo Oasis, which you'll be familiar with."

"Yes, deep inside Libya. A very handy base. It's within striking distance of the coast and the airfields."

"Indeed. And we've had word that Reid has captured it. Now Reid has orders to attack Axis supply columns in support of our counter thrust against Rommel, but the LRDG have also been asked to go after the airfields."

Stirling could scarcely contain himself. "That should be our job, sir."

"Calm yourself. The LRDG themselves have suggested you're better equipped for this, so the job is yours."

McDuff felt a growing excitement. This was it, the chance to strike and he couldn't contain himself. "Just the job, sir," he said. "We'll give them hell."

"I see your men are as bloodthirsty as you, David. Well, what do you say?"

"I say yes," Stirling said fervently. "We will raise bloody hell given the chance. And the LRDG will guide us?"

"Yes, your 'taxi service' has been confirmed. Now we just need to know which targets to hit."

"Yes, which of the airfields has the most value? Where are the enemy planes located that will inflict the most damage?"

"Precisely. And that is the intelligence we need and which we are waiting for. I've been told we should have it in the next day or so." Morris stood to signal the meeting was over. "So gather your wolves, David, it's time to go hunting. Get them ready, and we'll send word on where the sheep are waiting.

4

Emily Daws wondered what she looked like to the casual observer as she climbed the steps to the new library in Benghazi. It was one of the many public works projects that the then Governor-General, Italo Balbo, had commissioned during the wave of Italian immigration during the previous decade. It had the imposingly martial façade of classical Italy, wide steps leading to the grand brass doorway, ornately carved with mythical figures from African and Roman history. Several columns flanked the entrance, reaching high into the air where the architrave supported a frieze that had boldly inscribed in Latin the date of its founding and a call to the enduring power of education. Although perhaps not for the locals, Emily reflected.

Her shirt was stuck to her back by the time she arrived. Since she'd begun the walk from her lodgings, her pulse had steadily increased until, as she entered the darker interior, it was a trapped bird frantically seeking escape. It was markedly cooler inside as she headed towards the reception desk, giving her some relief. A fan lazily rotated in the lobby. She smiled at the solider and receptionist who manned the semi-circular front desk, fearing they could see how stricken she felt as she scrawled her name in the visitor's book. Since arriving in Benghazi she'd been a frequent visitor here, spending afternoons browsing the stacks of books; they were all government approved so the variety had not appealed. Yet it was necessary to establish herself here, as this was the location of her dead drop for passing on information to Alexandria. Though she was trained in wireless operation, it was felt too risky to provide her a transmitter, not least as she shared her lodgings which were always under some sort of surveillance. Thus, it had been agreed to revert to the old fashioned means of communicating. She'd never met whoever received and passed on her instructions in the library, and she hoped she never would. Each time she visited, her fear was a bitter taste in her mouth, her sweat an uncontrollable reaction to the gnawing sense of impending catastrophe. Who would be lying in wait for her? And each time she emerged, blinking into the fierce sunshine, she shaded her eyes and headed for the nearest bar for a drink.

She ascended the stairs, her shoes making a slight squeak on the polished floor as she pirouetted up to the next set of stairs, gripping the bannister tightly. The wood was smoothed by the passage of hands of researchers, readers and civil servants. Occasionally, she glanced down through the metal spindles, checking to see if anyone was following her. On the first floor a display created by the Libyan Colonisation Society proudly chronicled the history of Italian Libya, from the conquest in 1911 through to today. It made much of the origins of the name under the Emperor Diocletian, and bombastically claimed a promised land for colonists. Pictures of happy farmers working their olive groves were juxtaposed with the road building projects that had been initiated, all under the banner of progress. She rather doubted the locals who had been evicted and seen the best land given to Italians would agree and passed on by, heading to the top floor.

She cautiously opened the heavy door that led to the reference and research section, dedicated to both the history of the Italian people in Africa and the role and place of the native people in it. Weighty tomes lined the shelves, gathering dust. It was an ideal location for her drop. As an area of government focus and special policy – the pacification of local people and the promotion of a fascist ideology of Italian and Aryan supremacy – it was impeccably respectable for her to be here. Just as importantly, since many people here wore the mantle of Italian fascism lightly, it was nearly always empty. She glanced around but it was blessedly quiet. Very carefully she began to edge her way towards the far end, feeling the uncomfortable rasp of paper against her inner thigh where the report she had written lay. She had a sudden fear she may have sweated through the page, and the idea of going through what she had to get the information made her nauseous.

Her instructions from Alexandria had been, for once, specific. Decoding the message in the safety of the toilet in her flat, she'd lit a cigarette, her hands trembling slightly as she inhaled sharply. She burnt the paper, flushing the ashes down the loo and for a moment she sat there, feeling the terror that swam through her. Up until now, what she had sent back had been opportunistic and infrequent information she had either coaxed out of an unwary Major Rossi or seen from the papers she'd been asked to transcribe. One thing Major Rossi couldn't resist was an opportunity to boast and his in-built sense of superiority over a woman led him to frequent indiscretion.

"I am worried, Major," she'd breathed one afternoon. "Not long ago the British were here, and I can't help think what will come of us if it happens again."

"Do not worry, yourself, Angelina," Rossi said benevolently, leaning back to puff on his habitual cigar. "The proud fighting men of the Italian Army will force the enemy back and conquer Egypt, of that I am certain!"

"Do you really think so?"

"I know so! Every day our army grows and gets stronger. Our best divisions are arriving, and it can only be a matter of time before you and I are dining in the finest restaurants in Alexandria."

"A lovely thought, Major. I wish I had your confidence. Perhaps it is the weakness of a woman, but I do worry so."

"It is natural, but you are braver than most, just by being here."

"Thank you, Major. Not as brave as the fighting men, of course. Who are our finest divisions? I would love to learn of them."

Major Rossi frowned slightly. "These are confidential matters, Senorita."

"I apologise, Major. I simply wish to pray for them."

"And they would be worthy of your prayers." He leant forward conspiratorially. Emily had to force herself not to recoil. This was one of Rossi's favoured tricks, getting close to impart something secret. "Now, you must promise this is between you, I and God."

"Of course, Major."

Rossi lifted a finger. "I must be sure of you,

Senorita," he said sternly.

"You may depend on me."

"I do and I feel we must continue to work closely together. For the good of the nation."

Emily noted that Rossi had shifted his legs, a sign of his arousal. Swallowing her revulsion, she nodded demurely. "For Il Duce and Italy."

The mention of Mussolini prompted Rossi to sigh. He modelled himself explicitly on the leader, clothing himself in black and mimicking his speaking style. His paunch strained against his uniform and his imagined élan was a source of much mirth among the staff, as was his parroting of the tedious regime slogans. Emily was astonished he was in the position he was, but loyalty to the regime came with reward, and Rossi had been an early supporter of Mussolini. "Such a great man. An example to us all. And now, in his wisdom, we hear the news we have all been waiting for. Who will come to our aid to fight the British? Il Duce sends us his best. The famous Trieste division."

Emily's eyes widened slightly. "An elite force," she whispered. "Surely, they will turn the tide. I will pray for them."

Rossi patted her knee, his hand lingering. "And by doing so, you will help our cause."

And thus, she was able to report to Alexandria that the Trieste division was arriving in North Africa. She wasn't sure what happened to her missives, but she felt a fierce thrill that she was helping the war effort.

Yet the information she had been asked to source would require more than flattery and flirting. And that spelt danger. She needed to know where the Axis aircraft were concentrated, with particular reference to fighter dispositions. Information on

German targets would be more valuable than Italian. She knew that Rossi was privy to everything she needed but it wasn't something that could be wheedled out of him through flattery. It was contained in the safe in the corner of his office and she needed to see it, memorise it, encode it and send it. Fast.

The simplest route to the safe was to gain access while Major Rossi was absent. This happened frequently. Sometimes, he would slip out for a lingering lunch, at other times simply to stroll around the base, smoking. But a man only made it so far in a fascist state by being careful, and his safe was always kept locked. One afternoon, the Major excused himself and Emily sprang into action. Moving behind Rossi's desk, she began rapidly opening draws, looking under papers and books for any sign of a spare key. Nothing. Her palms were sticky with sweat and she could feel her pulse beating in her throat. Rossi could be back any moment. She straightened, glancing outside but no one was paying attention and she carefully half closed the blinds. Turning, she moved toward to the filing cabinets, testing a few drawers. Several were locked, and a cursory look at the others revealed administrative paperwork only. She despaired. Where would he put a spare key? How long did she have? She looked back at the desk. She got down on her hands and knees, looking for any secret compartments, running her hand along the edges. Again, nothing. She started thinking of any other places when a voice sounded, sending a shiver of panic flooding through her.

"What are you doing?"

Looking out under the desk, she saw a pair of sensible shoes and a woman's sturdy calves covered by light stockings. She cursed. Maria Garavellli ran the secretarial pool and was a humourless, efficient woman who ran the office like a fiefdom.

Emily began to rise, banging her head on the edge of the desk, bringing tears to her eyes. It helped explain the flush in her face that had risen at the sound of Garavelli's voice, but it also gave her a jolt of anger. In a moment of fear and inspiration, she ripped one of her earrings off and clutched it her hand. She struggled to her feet and held it open. "I'm sorry, Miss Garavelli, I lost an earring," she said, holding it out in her hand.

"Where is Major Rossi?"

"He just stepped out."

"You shouldn't be in here alone. And how did your earring get there?"

Emily stared back at Garavelli. How indeed? "Well, the Major often needs me here," she said carefully and then began to blush by thinking about what she and a French airman had gotten up to in an Anderson shelter during a raid last year. "You see, sometimes we work closely together, and he can be, well, very attentive…" Her voice trailed off and she looked imploringly at Garavelli.

Even Garavelli recoiled at the implication and her voice hardened. "You stupid girl. And regardless, this is still unacceptable."

At that moment, Major Rossi appeared at the door. "What's this? Two beautiful women in my office? An auspicious day!"

"Major, this girl was in here unaccompanied and under your desk. This is a breach of protocol and must be reported."

Rossi waved a hand dismissively, taking his seat. "Your dedication to your duty is admirable, Miss Garavelli. However, my secretary has my confidence.

Why were you under my desk, Angelina?"

"I lost an earring, Major," Emily said demurely.

"See? Nothing to worry yourself over."

"But Major, this is – "

"Not now, Miss Garavelli," Major Rossi cut her off. "I will deal with this. You may go."

Garavelli glared at Emily before nodding. "As you wish."

Rossi gave Emily a mock stern look. "Now, now, Angelina. You must not embarrass me so."

"I'm so sorry, Major. These were given to me by my mother."

"Ah, a lovely sentimental heirloom." Rossi advanced, cupping Emily's ear as he examined the earring. "They are beautiful and made more so by their wearer." He beamed, his gin laced breath wafting over here. "We have much in common, and could be good for each other, but we must be careful, yes?"

Once Emily's pulse returned to normal, she'd spent the rest of the day worrying at the problem. Even if she succumbed to Rossi's advances, she had no illusions that would give her access to the safe. Besides, there was only so much one was willing to do for King and country. Yet she needed that information. And more than that, she wanted to succeed. This was her first real assignment and she had to get it right.

The next day, her spirits flagged as it felt like there was no prospect of getting into the safe. She'd tried to see the combination code when Rossi used it, but he always kept the safe covered when he opened it and she daren't not seem too interested. For once, Major Rossi was in business like mood. A meeting was being held with the senior officers of the Corps, and Major Rossi was due to present a summary of his intelligence findings the next day. He was in irritable mood, clearly under pressure but it had focused him. From early morning he had dictated notes, letters and reports to Emily, sending her to other departments to get more reports, and giving every impression of effective administration. He occasionally referred to the contents of his safe, taking Emily's drafts and adding final figures that were secret, or adding in the details of his intelligence sources. One thing that Emily was sure of, was that whatever Rossi would present, it would be carefully constructed to protect the Major and the SIM whatever the outcome. The problem was that Rossi seemed chained to his desk, snapping out orders and making phone calls. She needed a way of getting rid of Rossi and doing so fast, so that he would forget to lock the safe. She racked her brains as the day wore on. What did Rossi fear? What motivated him? The idea that came to her was simple, reckless and unreliable but it was all she had.

As the day wore on, the office quietened, and she decided she had to risk it. Coming back from collecting another report, she approached Rossi's desk with the file. "I just saw Colonel Ferroni's secretary," she said, handing over the file. "She said something I found strange - I know you mentioned you were unsure of the man, I'm not sure if it's anything at all…"

Major Rossi's head whipped up at the mention of Ferroni. "You may speak freely here, Angelina, and in strictest confidence. What did you hear?"

"That Colonel Ferroni has uncovered something big and was on his way to the General right now to inform him."

Rossi frowned. "Hmm. I wonder what that is."

"Well, that's the thing. She also said Ferroni

was boasting on the phone that it wouldn't be good news for 'Rossi and his lot.'"

Rossi was standing now, his senses on alert. His resentment at Ferroni and OVRA had fed into a paranoia that he was being investigated. "When was this?"

"Just now, Major. Apparently, the Colonel had just left when I arrived."

"Damn that man." Rossi rose, visibly agitated, yanking down his uniform and grabbing his cap. "Continue with the report – I must nip this in the bud or they'll be trouble for all of us."

Rossi marched out, leaving Emily standing before the desk. This was the moment of truth. When Rossi realised there was no such plan, he would return immediately, and she knew she had a matter of moments. Was the safe unlocked? Before she lost her nerve, she moved swiftly to the safe, kneeling before it. With trembling fingers, she grasped the handle and pulled. To her joy and intense relief, it opened. She quickly scanned the documents inside. One of the reports she had read referenced a summary of aircraft dispositions – she knew it was here. Frantically, she flicked through the reports and files contained, careful to keep them in order. Where was it? Come on, come on, she thought. She was running out of time and beginning to despair, when a phrase caught her eye on one of the documents she had passed – Regio Aeronautica. Rapidly bringing it out, she almost sobbed in relief. Her blood raged inside her and she took two deep breaths to calm her nerves. She had to remember this. Scanning the pages, she knew she had what she needed so, taking a moment, she concentrated and began to memorise what she saw.

She had learnt many memory tricks from her father, and they served her well. One was pegging – imagining a coat peg in your mind when remembering words or phrases, and 'hooking' them onto the peg. Thus, she had five pegs in her mind, one each for the airfields at Sirte, Tamet, Nofilia, Aghelia and Agedabia. Then there was reduction. For German aircraft of the same manufacturer – such as the Messerschmitt whose planes were abbreviated to ME – she simply noted in her mind the final numerical designator. Thus, on the neatly typed page, 12 ME109s at Sirte airfield, became SME912, while five ME110s at Tamet became TME510 and so on. She followed the same scheme for the Italian planes. Yet there was a real difference in remembering a poem with her father compared to acting as a spy in the office on an enemy officer, and she kept closing her eyes as the numbers slipped away from her.

Finally, she felt she had it and closed the safe, standing and smoothing her skirt before walking briskly to her desk just outside Major Rossi's office. It was not a moment too soon, as a perplexed Major Rossi returned.

"Colonel Ferroni was in his office."

"Oh. Perhaps he had already been?"

"No, I checked with the General's staff. He is elsewhere today."

Rossi stared at Emily, frowning and Emily forced herself to speak calmly. "Mischief making? That secretary is a notorious gossip."

Rossi looked into his office. He seemed to be considering and Emily said a silent prayer. Just as Rossi was about to speak, the phone rang, and she gratefully answered it. "Major Rossi's office? Yes, I have him here." She handed the receiver to Rossi. "It's the cipher section, sir. Do you wish to take it?"

Rossi nodded and sat down. "Put them through. And please finish the report."

Emily smiled and left. She sat down at her desk as Rossi went back to his desk, closing the door behind him. She felt sick and it was the memory of that nausea that now stalked her as she inched her way towards the dead drop. The idea of going through that again was unconscionable, at least anytime soon. She prayed again that her report had not been ruined as it lay secure against her thigh. The rest of the day had been torture. Every time Rossi opened his door she trembled, expecting a summons, followed by an accusation and her inevitable discovery. Yet judging from the sounds from the office, of slamming receivers and shouts for more information, Rossi had the next day's meeting firmly in his mind. And the agonising minutes passed by, until finally she was able to leave and return to her lodgings. Arriving home, she ran into one of her housemates, who stopped her on the stairs.

"Hey, Angelina, you look awful? You ok?"

"It's nothing," Emily mumbled. "Wrong food."

"Ah, know the feeling. Get well soon!"

Settling in her room, she had encoded her report using the poem cipher system – the poem, known to her and Peter in Alexandria, was used to both generate the key and encode the message. Her chosen poem was Daffodils by Wordsworth, a choice Peter had approved of. It was time consuming and her attention to detail had to be spot on – a single error would render the message unreadable. Whilst it was a fairly basic means of coding, it was simple to learn and needed no equipment. She was left with a message of meaningless letters in five letter groups which she folded up and slipped into her knickers, breathing a huge sigh of relief as she carefully hid it in the depths of her wardrobe. Only then could she collapse on the bed, feeling almost ready to cry such was the release of fear and joy. She slept deeply that night, and in the morning set out for the library. She kept glancing back over her shoulder to see if she was being followed, before berating herself for acting suspiciously. By the time she arrived, she was in turmoil but finally, she came to the last row in the reference section. There, she carefully lifted off a couple of books, browsing them, almost expecting a hand to grasp her by the shoulder and haul her off. But nothing stirred, and so she gently took out La Dottrina del Fascismo. She smiled – it was a treatise written by Mussolini himself. It was drivel and she was sure there would be no one taking it out here. She had carefully slit open the glue on the back cover to leave a small crack, into which she now carefully placed the folded notepaper. Carefully putting the book back, she rested her hand on the spine and said a brief prayer. For the first time, she felt like a real spy. She'd been given a dangerous task and she had delivered. And now it was time to find a drink.

5

It had only been two weeks since the abortive raid on the airfields, but McDuff felt an undercurrent of excitement and determination running through the camp. Upon their return from Alexandria, Stirling had immediately ordered that they pack up and head the several hundred miles east to Jalo Oasis. They'd not had time to dwell on the failure of the previous raid and the men were heartened by McDuff's account of his trip with Stirling.

"Honestly, I thought they were going to can the lot of us," he recounted, sitting round his tent brewing up. The light was fading, and a small group of expectant men were gathered round.

"What did they say?"

"Oh, that the whole thing was a disaster, and that the SAS weren't the sort of rabble the British Army was looking for."

"In fairness, we are a rabble," someone remarked. "Don't think Hanson's seen a shower in months."

"Glass houses, Pete," Hanson replied.

"The ugliest bunch of bastards this side of Cairo."

"Told them straight up we were on," McDuff continued. "And, in the right conditions, we'd be fine."

"Too right. Won't get a storm like that again."

"Yep. They didn't like it but basically, there's a flap going on with the Eighth and Rommel and they aren't worried about the likes of us lot right now. So we've got another chance." McDuff smiled fiercely. "So we're on. Another go at the airfields."

They'd wound and bumped their way through the desert to reach Jalo Oasis, a grim and wearying journey as all desert travel was. Finally, they'd arrived and, as they crested a small rise, came to a brief halt above the oasis. "Like a picture book," Hanson murmured, and McDuff agreed. A vast pool of glittering water lay at Jalo's heart, several miles wide and long. It was fringed by palm trees that waved back and forth in the wind. Ahead of them was a large, irregularly shaped fort, its white walls showing starkly in the sun. Whoever controlled it, controlled the oasis. And with it, came a very useful strategic base for desert operations. As each side advanced up the coastal strip, Jalo had to be taken and it would be fought over time and again.

The land was sandy and undulating with various small clumps of huts, wells and pumpkin patches dotted around. On the fort's longest wall was the main gate and along its crenelated top, a sentry could be glimpsed walking up and down. Their little convoy wound its way down the track, passing by several camels and through the doors which swung open as they approached. The fort was scarred from Brigadier Reid's assault, black pockmarks from gun fire showing clearly against the whitewashed walls and in one corner a partial collapse which was under repair. A burnt-out armoured car rested under the walls and several of the mud houses that the local Berbers lived in had been destroyed. One Berber stood, motionless as they passed, holding a camel. His face was obscured by his dark blue headdress and his blank eyes made McDuff shiver; the man and his people had seen the likes of McDuff come and go again and again.

He turned back to the fort as they pulled in, laagering their trucks and jumping down, and it was only when they were stationary that the illusion of a beautiful oasis began to dissipate. The full force of the heat hit them immediately. At least when they were travelling, they had some kind of breeze to cool them, but it was roastingly hot in the fort. "Christ," McDuff muttered as he gathered his weapon and jumped down. The heat was a wall. It felt like he was walking in sludge as he looked around, and even inside the fort a ravening wind tore at him. As he turned, he sensed a movement out of the corner of his eye and then felt something land on his face. "Flies," he said in disgust. Beside him, Hanson was waving his hands and tucking his headdress more firmly over his face, as swarms of fat, black flies buzzed around them. "They're everywhere," he said and hurried towards the shaded colonnade.

As they moved forward, Captain Stirling emerged, waving them over. He'd gone ahead of them to prepare and he was bouncing. "Over here, gentlemen. Time for your orders."

McDuff felt a tingle of excitement. "Here we go," he said tightly, and Hanson gave him a thumbs up. Stirling had set up his command post in a disused storehouse and they gathered round expectantly. He was flanked by Lewes, Paddy Mayne and Bill Fraser, an enigmatic Scotsman who'd missed the first raid due to a broken wrist. He was a quiet man but respected for his granite resolve and stamina. At his feet, his dog, Withers, lay panting.

Stirling looked around. "What happened last month was a tragedy. Good men were lost, men who had so much to offer. None of us could ever have foreseen that that would be the outcome of our first mission."

The men were sombre. Hanson, who'd lost a good friend in the raid, whispered angrily to McDuff. "Why's he bringing this up?" McDuff didn't reply. Hanson was dealing with his loss by not thinking about it, and who was he to argue.

"But that wasn't because this idea can't work. That wasn't because the enemy were better than us. That wasn't because we weren't well trained enough or strong enough. We operate in the Devils' country and that night he was in charge." He paused, taking in the young, tanned faces that looked back at him. "But the Devil has had his time. We're going back to those airfields. We won't face a storm. We won't fail the mission. And this time, we will be the devil and any Jerry or Eyetie in the way is going to suffer the wrath of the Special Air Service."

McDuff cheered along with the rest of them. "This is it," he shouted to Hanson. "This time we do it right." It summed up the mood of the men; eager not just to succeed, but to prove that the failure of the first raid was God's and God's alone, not the SAS.

Stirling raised his hands for silence. "And what we know now is where our prizes lie. Before we set out, I received the news we need, that of the enemy dispositions. People have risked their lives for that information," he warned, "so let's make this count. It tells us where our prizes lie, where the blow will fall that will most humble the enemy. Our targets are the major airfields at Sirte, Aghelia and Agedabia. I will lead the team attacking Sirte; Lieutenant Lewes will attack Aghelia the same night, and finally, Lieutenant Fraser will take Agedabia. We leave in three days."

There was an excited murmur as the men broke up, spreading out to find their quarters and prepare for dinner – bully beef, biscuits, dried bread and yams. The flies buzzed around them incessantly and the men ate quickly. Not that they needed any encouragement. "I'm starving," McDuff said in the silence which settled over the group as they wolfed down the dinner. They were constantly hungry, and sources of food were a ceaseless speculation. They'd been hopeful rumours of captured Italian supplies, but the haul had been meagre and already picked over by Brigadier Reid's force. Even worse, the oasis, which looked so inviting, was brackish and salty, and mosquitos and flies plagued them when they went close. In the end, it was a relief when Lieutenant Lewes had summoned McDuff to his tent.

"Come with me, Sergeant. I've been working on a solution to one of our munitions challenges and you're going to help me solve it."

He strode out of the fort, McDuff hurrying to keep up. "Munitions challenge?"

"Yes. It's a question of chemistry. If we are to be effective in destroying the enemy's aircraft, our sabotage equipment must explode and ignite. We need to ignite the fuel tanks, thus ending in a detonation that meets our objective. With me so far?"

"Yes, sir."

"Good. And, of course, it has to be portable. Know what that means?"

"We need to be able to carry enough of them, easily, to destroy as many aircraft as possible."

"Quite. And the ones we've been forced to use until now have essentially been two bombs in one – so they're cumbersome and that's no good. I've been designing my own version and we're going to perfect it this afternoon. Here, take these."

Lewes handed over the canvas bags he was carrying, and McDuff peered inside. "What's in here, sir?"

"Gelignite for the explosive; detonators, ammonal, gun cotton and other bits and pieces, such as thermite, for ignition."

"And the gun oil to make it stick?"

"Precisely. Now, we just need to work out the final proportions. Which is where you come in."

McDuff wondered precisely what that meant but Lewes had halted some distance into the desert. A table had been set up next to a large boulder and Lewes directed McDuff to set up their equipment there. A hundred yards away was the rusting wreck of a lorry. "Our target," Lewes indicated at the rock. "Our cover," gesturing at the boulder. They proceeded to carefully arrange all the required materials in front of them. "The key is the proportions. Your job is to copy my lead but using slightly different proportions. That way, we shall arrive at the required levels. Clear?"

McDuff nodded, and began to copy Lewes as he constructed the first bomb. McDuff followed as closely as he could, mildly terrified he was about to blow his arm off, but also excited. They'd been working on just such a bomb and if Lewes had finally perfected it, it would be invaluable. "Like this?" he queried.

"Yes, but I want your one to use quarter pound of

plastic explosive first up, with an eighth of a pound of thermite. We'll take it in turns to place the bomb and time the detonation."

McDuff nodded and rolled thermite and explosive together with the motor oil. The effect was to produce something that resembled a black pudding. A pencil detonator, a glass tube the size of a pen, would be used to control the time the bomb took to detonate – when the glass was squeezed, it released acid which ate its way through a copper wire to reach the explosive mix. The speed of detonation depended on the thickness of the wire, and the only way to know for sure was to experiment with different thicknesses.

Lewes went first, heading out to the wreck and placing the bomb carefully on what remained of the bonnet. "When I shout, start timing," he said to McDuff, then squeezed the phial and hurried back. "Now!" He arrived back and they waited expectantly. "Primed it for what should be two minutes," he said.

Two minutes came and went. Lewes frowned. Another thirty seconds passed.

"Maybe it's a dud?" McDuff ventured, but at that moment, a dull bang sounded, and the bomb went up. He and Lewes went over to examine the damage, which was not nearly as much as they'd expected.

"Poor ignition and not as much damage as I'd hope. And it took longer than expected. So more of everything and less wire this time, McDuff."

McDuff complied, raising the levels of thermite and explosive, and using a thinner section of wire. Once he had the bomb ready, he glanced at Lewes who nodded, and McDuff walked out towards the car, again aiming for two minutes and attaching it firmly to the skeleton.

He'd only just reached the cover of the boulder

when an enormous explosion ripped out. The table was blown over and the wash of the concussion even reached them by the boulder. "Too much," Lewes muttered, standing up and brushing himself down. He reached out a hand to pull McDuff up to his feet. "Right. I think we've got it now and at least we know what thirty seconds looks like."

Over the next few hours, McDuff and Lewes experimented with varying combinations of ingredients, placements and fuses. McDuff's hands grew filthy, as did his shorts which he was constantly wiping. He began to feel nauseous from the fumes and the sky was darkening when Lewes finally declared himself satisfied. Taking the final bomb, he took it to the skeletal remains of the vehicle and placed it reverently, before calmly walking back after squeezing the detonating phial. What remained of the vehicle was obliterated and McDuff emerged, grinning. "A lovely bang, sir," he said.

"A very effective detonation, indeed, Sergeant."

"And a lovely weapon. We should call it the 'Lewes Bomb.'"

"Its name is not as important, as long as it does its job."

The next day was spent preparing for the journey and the raid. McDuff had been allocated to Captain Stirling's raiding party which he was pleased about. They attended several briefings focused on the enemy dispositions and defences, which were expected to be relatively light. A lot of focus was on what to do if the raid went wrong, and where they were to head to if they were split up. The Long Range Desert Group attended many of the sessions, as they were the final, integral part of the plan. They had been operating in the desert since June 1940 and were a relaxed and competent outfit, with their own mores, slang and easy familiarity. They'd been providing vital intelligence and information on the enemy ever since their formation, and were unparalleled in navigating, hiding in and traversing the desert spaces. McDuff envied and admired them. "There's nothing they don't know about the desert," he observed after being given a thorough description and analysis of the route they were going to take to the coast and the airfields.

Gazing out over the bustling activity in the fort, McDuff thought the two groups – the LRDG and the SAS – couldn't be further from the image of a British Army unit. Nearly all had bushy beards and leathery faces, the wrinkles from squinting etched outside their eyes. Arab headdresses abounded, useful for cover against flies and flying sand, and the standard army boots had long been discarded in favour of desert sandals, known as chapplies, which much lighter and cooler on the feet. All of them wore a scarf to protect their face from sand and dust, and MT goggles were ubiquitous, slung around the neck or resting on their forehead. The dress varied according to taste. Some of the men were in standard olive brown Battle Dress, while others had adopted the lighter Khaki Dress long sleeve shirt and shorts. Webley .45s were worn on the hip by many, alongside their usual weapons, a mixture of SMLE rifles and Thompson machine guns. These were constantly tended to by the men, requiring regular cleaning - the desert got into every nook and cranny of weapons and men, causing misfires in combat that could be deadly, and sores and lice in the men that were a source of constant irritation. On patrol, it was forbidden to use water for personal hygiene so the first thing the men usually did was have a good shave and clean when they returned; by now, they were ready to go back, and were looking as villainous as any comic book imagination could conjure. McDuff smiled; they looked brilliant.

He joined the men who had gathered round a desert stove to brew up. The stove was a simple but effective tool; the troopers would take a drum and punch some holes in it for ventilation, before filling it with sand and adding petrol. Tea or food could be placed directly on the heated sand to heat it. Gratefully, he sipped the tea as the sun dipped beneath the horizon, thinking on the morrow. It would be his chance to finally engage the enemy and he felt a tremor of fear and excitement at the thought.

"Not long now," Hanson said.

McDuff nodded and gazed out into the desert night, thinking of the moors of Cumbria, the untamed landscape, beautiful, rugged and dangerous. So like to the desert, yet so different. And thinking of tomorrow. "We're a long way from home," he said.

"Yeah, but I'd rather be here than back in London getting bombed."

"No doubt. The bastards aren't going to know what's hit them."

"Yep. Wouldn't want to be in their shoes when 'L' Detachment shows up."

"One look at you would be enough to frighten the poor bastards to death."

Hanson grinned. "That's going to be the least of their worries."

McDuff drained his tea, laced with a friendly ration of rum, feeling the warmth spreading inside him, along with his own building excitement. "Right, I'm off my beauty sleep."

The men from LRDG and 'L' Detachment rose well before dawn, finalising all the myriad details that were needed for their trek across the desert. They were 350 miles from the coast and the airfields, and it would take three days to reach their targets. Gathering around their vehicles, they made their final preparations. Only what was absolutely vital could be taken with them, and their transport reflected the combined experience of pre-war desert travel and that of the LRDG. Their main transport was several Chevrolet trucks, adapted and repurposed for desert warfare. As he swung up a jerrycan of spare petrol into the flatbed in the back, McDuff paused to wipe the sweat from his brow, and took in the rugged Chevy upon which his survival depended.

When traversing the desert, weight was everything and the Chevy had been stripped of absolutely anything that was superfluous to operational need. The doors were gone, as were the cab roof and windscreen, both to reduce weight but also minimise the risk of the sun glinting off it and giving their position away. Even the rear-view mirror was taken out. Holes were cut into the triangular shaped bonnet to allow greater circulation of air to the engine, which was itself modified with a larger radiator and condenser system. On the back, a wooden truck bed was built on the superstructure and hanging off the side were numerous storage bins, containing maps, ammunition, rations, tents and camouflage netting. McDuff noted the containers above the wheel arches of the specially modified tyres – they were wider than normal tyres with reduced pressure that spread out and gripped the sand better. In the bins was the 'unsticking gear' – the sand mats and sand channels needed when the vehicles were bogged down. It was backbreaking work but vital if they were to make it through the desert.

McDuff reached out a hand and Hanson swung him into the back of the truck. Between the jerry cans of petrol and water and spare tyres, there wasn't much room for the men. There was no roof, and the men had to make themselves as comfortable as they could. McDuff edged past the swan mounted Vickers .303 machine gun which constituted the main armament of the truck; it could traverse around them and offered some protection against aerial threat, although the best defence against planes was simply to hide.

Leaning forward, McDuff peered into the cab. A Lewes machine gun provided forward defence and firepower, and personal rifles were fixed by a clip to the back of the cab. He nodded to a tall New Zealander, who would be their navigator for the journey. "All ok?"

"All set, pommie. Your taxi is ready to go."

"Glad to hear it," McDuff grinned. "And glad you're driving me, not me."

"Ah, the desert's a lady if you know how to work with her."

"Well, as long as you reckon you can drop us off right on the dot, we'll do the rest."

"I think we'll be ok." The man had an understated but entirely believable confidence. The LRDG had pioneered all sorts of navigational aids to help them travers the desert, often invented by their founder, Major Bagnold, an engineer veteran of the first war. He had had made the first recorded east to west crossing of the Libyan Desert and among his legacies was a sun compass unaffected by metal and therefore not affected by magnetism in the desert. It was affixed to the dashboard and the driver gave it an affectionate pat. "We'll get you there, Pom."

"Make sure you do, pal." McDuff patted him on the shoulder and turned back, taking in the activity as the final checks were made to their convoy. Each of the trucks was painted in a mix of hues of pink and grey, and the harsh wind whipped the pennant on the lead truck. The unyielding sun beat down on them and McDuff took a deep breath of dry air. He saw Stirling exchange a handshake with Lewes and then hop into his truck. It was time. McDuff sat down and closed his eyes. They were going to cross Devil's Country, find the enemy asleep and vulnerable in their beds, and bring fire and fury out of the desert night. The pirates were out, the enemy were waiting, and the SAS were going to join the fight.

6

The convoy snaked out through the Libyan desert, the bone-dry wind scorching the men as they swayed wearily in the back of the trucks. Their water was strictly rationed, and the sweat that sprung out on their foreheads dried instantly, leaving a fine, salty crust on their faces. McDuff pulled his headdress tighter around his face, squinting against the fierce glare of the sun. Pulling his goggles down more firmly to give him respite against the wind-whipped sand, he shifted to try and get more comfortable. The trucks were built for durability, not comfort, and the men were bounced around in the back, bumping into their neighbour or being thrown forward as they took another dip or rise. They jolted over the landscape, occasionally entering a hidden gully or wadi, engine working to drive the trucks up each slight incline. Sometimes, they came close to small settlements, little more than a few huts and tents, but usually they avoided the local populace. It was a shadow world where spies from each side operated, and the locals were loyal to their own tribe and would gladly play one side off against the other. Conversation was muted, each man weighed down by the soporific motion of the truck and the harsh heat that drained a man of energy. The wooden benches in the truck dug into their thighs, leaving red creases on the skin that if left unattended could fester and turn into sores. The sun, unblinking in the sky, incessantly beat down and they broiled in the heat of the day, as sand whipped up by the stiff wind coated every inch of exposed skin.

"Devil country," McDuff grunted, and Hanson nodded. They were fighting the land before they could fight the enemy, but the land was unyielding, and their endurance was being put to the test. The truck suddenly came to a juddering halt and McDuff groaned. The first time they had bogged down, McDuff tackled the task of digging out with determination. This was the third time, and he was beginning to see the merits of the parachute insertion method again. Jumping wearily down, he opened the storage bin over the wheel, taking out the sand mats and heading to the front of the truck. He inspected the wheels with the driver. They were deeply embedded in the cloying sand, spinning uselessly as they couldn't get purchase. "Gonna need some digging, Pom," the driver observed, pushing back the distinctive campaign hat that marked him out as a New Zealander. "A lot of digging."

McDuff, Hanson and the others took turns to dig under the trapped truck. It was back breaking work, their torment made worse by the heat. Sweat poured down their backs and chests, sand sticking to them and working its way into their clothes, so they always felt a little itchy. They panted in the heat as they took shifts, attacking the sand before the next man began. "Christ," gasped McDuff as he staggered to the back of the truck after one such effort, one hand holding the truck for support. "Bloody sand."

Eventually, the sand mats would be placed

under the wheels, and the driver would gently gun the engine to move onto them, until the wheels found traction and lurched forward onto better ground again. The men would climb back in the truck and the whole process would begin again. Jolting along, praying they wouldn't have to stop again, only to hear the curse of the driver that signalled a burst tyre. Rousing themselves, they rolled one of the spares off the back of the truck, taking the chance to brew up with their desert stoves and munch of a date as the new tyre was fixed in. The old tyre was taken with them and they set off again, trusting the LRDG to take them where they needed to go. Yet even as the sun finally began to relent and dip below the horizon, there was little respite from the desert. The men immediately began to shiver as the temperature plummeted. As they laagered for the night, throwing over their camouflage netting and preparing a warm meal, they huddled in their greatcoats, waiting for the escape of sleep.

"Crikey, it's freezing," Hanson said, his teeth chattering.

"Have some of this, it'll help." One of the LRDG passed over a large jar, with the inscription 'SRD' stamped on its side. It sloshed as he passed it and a wonderful aroma wafted over them.

"SRD?" McDuff said as he waited for his turn, licking his lips in anticipation.

"Supply Reserve Depot. All sorts of stuff can go in there, but we prefer rum. Makes nights like this a little more bearable".

"Amen," McDuff replied, swallowing and feeling the heat spread inside him. "Amen."

Much later, McDuff took a watch and gazed out into the surrounding vastness. It felt like they were the only ones on earth, traversing an unknown and unkind world where only the foolhardy ventured. A look into the sky, his breath fogging against the brightest canopy of stars he'd ever seen, made his heart catch. The otherworldly beauty of the desert, so deadly, was hard to comprehend. And hard to think that soon they would be going into the white-hot intensity of combat. It would be his first real experience of war and he wondered how he would cope. Would he freeze? How would he manage the fear and what if he was wounded? It wasn't something to share with the other men, these were his own demons to fight and his excitement was laced with guilt and fear, fear of the enemy but also a fear he would let the men down, be found wanting. And so, as he stared into the bleak expanse before him, alone aside from the stars that serenely moved above him, he offered a short prayer; a prayer for courage, for luck and for his mates to come through unscathed.

The next day the convoy continued, grinding out mile after mile. They set off as dawn was rising and the sun quickly found them, turning its unflinching gaze onto them once more. They motored for several hours, passing wind-blown rock formations and scrubland. The overriding colour was brown, but multiple shades and hues. Darker toned rock formations that had baked in the sun for a hundred years lay alongside the rust coloured sand dunes that flowed into undulating golden-brown plains. The occasional hardy acacia and scrub broke the flatland with their dour colouring and above it all, the bluest of blue skies reigned. McDuff closed his eyes against the heat, passing the time thinking of the mission, the plan of attack and imagining the fear of the enemy – as much to give him comfort.

Yet once more their journey came to a halt when a sharp bang sounded from one of the trucks. Immediately, a belching cloud of steam rose from the bonnet. The driver ran to the front of the truck, using a cloth to shield his hands from the scorching heat as he raised the bonnet high. He waved a hand to clear the smoke, peering inside and McDuff heard the man's curse from where he was. The convoy halted and a conference was held at the truck. Impatiently, McDuff waited, scanning the sky above. Their navigator had confirmed they were only seventy miles from the coast and well inside the operational sphere of enemy aircraft. They couldn't afford to be anchored out in the open for too long.

The truck's engine coughed, died and coughed again, spouting more smoke. McDuff willed it to come back; if they couldn't move it, it would need to be abandoned and, likely, some of their precious supplies left behind. Finally, to his intense relief the engine roared into life and they set off again, yet they'd scarcely gone half a mile before the truck began misfiring again and scalding hot steam was wafting over the cab. The driver leapt down again, signalling the convoy to stop but as he did so, a voice rang out urgently. "'Ware aircraft!" All heads turned skyward, seeing the dark spec coming closer to them. It was an Italian Ghibli reconnaissance plane and they were stranded in the open, impossible to miss.

"On the trucks!" The men scrambled, engines gunning, leaving the stricken truck behind. McDuff tensed as the plane came closer, feeling the nausea spreading as two little, dark shapes detached from the plane, wobbling down toward them, and McDuff found he was holding his breath until the bombs exploded harmlessly wide. "That won't be the last of them!" observed their driver as they halted while the aircraft disappeared over the horizon to summon reinforcements. Captain Stirling jumped down to confer with Mayne, Lewes and Fraser.

"They'll be after us now," he said without preamble. "We can split up and head to the road individually or try and hide it out." He shaded his eyes. "There's a patch of camel scrub up there we can use."

"It would be best to stay together," Lewes replied. "We can make time and they may not even be able to find us. It's simply a question of how long before their reinforcements get here."

"Agreed," Mayne said. "What about the truck?" he added, gesturing back to where the LRDG were still trying to coax it back to life.

McDuff had been listening to the exchange and cautiously cleared his throat. "Could we use it as bait?"

Stirling looked at him thoughtfully. "We'd lose a truck, but yes, that might work, Sergeant. It's probably US anyway. Quickly – head to the scrub, hide the trucks. Put the broken one at the north end and hide it, but not well. Let's see if we can draw their fire."

The men sprang into action and the convoy increased speed and headed for the scrub which was about half a mile in length. The dying truck was coaxed into gear and placed at the north end, while the men leapt down, spreading out across the rest of the scrub and frantically putting out the camouflage nets. Then they hid as best they could, waiting for the inevitable response.

It wasn't long in coming. McDuff lay panting in the heat, his heart in his mouth, feeling the helplessness as two more planes appeared, buzzing angrily in from the deep blue sky.

"Shouldn't we fire back?" Hanson asked

"No point," McDuff replied through gritted teeth. "Just have to hope the bastards miss."

The planes circled the area high overhead in a wide arc, sun winking off their metal fuselages, as they sought out the convoy. "Keep going, keep going," Hanson muttered, but the planes suddenly banked hard, their pilots heaving on the control stick and dove straight for the patch of scrub. The shrieking whine of their engines rose to a pitch as they homed in, pulling up to disgorge their payload, a row of explosions ripping through the scrub.

"They're taking the bait," McDuff shouted exultantly as the planes homed in on the far end of the shrub. They made several passes on it, but they hadn't forgotten the rest of the scrub. As they were strafed and bombed, McDuff was sure it was only a matter of time before someone or something was hit. He steeled himself for the screams and shouts he was sure to come. The planes banked round again, this time coming in low, the bark of their cannons echoing off the rocks. McDuff glimpsed the pilot as the plane flashed by, the man's face obscured by the goggles and breathing apparatus that lent him the look of an alien figure hunting them. McDuff followed the planes as they lazily completed another wide circle, before lining up for another attack. Again, the shrill whine of the engines built and built as the planes roared in for the attack; more dull concussions sounded, this time close to where McDuff sheltered, so close he felt the earth vibrate under his stomach. Warm sand sprayed across him and he buried his face in his arms, tasting sand on his lips. Raising his head a fraction, he noticed a small lizard hiding under a rock not far from his resting place. It's unblinking eye fixed on him as its flanks rose and fell to the rapid rhythm of its breathing, from fear or heat, McDuff was unsure. It started at each blast, and McDuff willed it to stay; if it stayed, he felt it would survive. He sensed something else, and glancing beyond the lizard, saw Lieutenant Mayne watching him with an amused half-smile on this face. To McDuff's astonishment, Mayne was reading a book.

"Not very accurate are they, Sergeant?" Mayne said laconically.

"Close enough for my liking, sir."

"They're guessing we're here, but the only thing they can glimpse is that truck and they're not even doing a very good job on it. Their bomb pattern is very wayward. We'll be on the move shortly."

"Crazy Mick," McDuff muttered, carefully so as not to be heard. Mayne's temperament was legendarily explosive, but McDuff took comfort from Mayne's coolness.

Sure enough, after fifteen minutes the planes turned and flew north, their dark specks receding rapidly into the distance. McDuff stood, brushing himself down and joined the others in uncovering their trucks. "Quickly now!" shouted Captain Stirling as he moved down the convoy. "And everyone keep your eyes open. We're getting close now."

McDuff shifted restlessly as they set out, keenly aware now that action was impending. His mouth felt even drier than normal, and he kept scanning the sky. Yet as the sun began to gracefully sink behind the horizon there were no further alarms and their LRDG guides pulled them up, announcing they were only four miles from the coast and the first of the targets, Sirte airfield. McDuff dropped down from the truck, wondering if it was his imagination or if he could catch a faint whiff of the sea. He stretched his back and began helping set the camp up for the evening, draping the trucks with camouflage, checking weapons and digging a temporary latrine pit. As he settled down with his evening meal of bully beef, biscuits, yams and dried bread, he noticed the officers were in a huddle and seemed to be holding an urgent debate.

"Wonder what's got their knickers in a twist," he remarked to Hanson, but it wasn't long for them to find out. Stirling approached them and held his hands out for silence.

"Change of plans, gentlemen. Since we've been spotted there's a risk that there will be increased security, especially Sirte which is so close. So we're going to break into two parties." He turned and gestured to Paddy Mayne. "Lieutenant Mayne will be leading a force that will head about thirty miles further along the coast to attack the airfield at Tamet, which we are expecting to be relatively lightly guarded, while my party will continue as planned to Sirte. We'll both attack tomorrow night and hopefully, at least one of us will get lucky. Questions?"

There were none and the men broke up, muttering quietly amongst themselves. "Not ideal," McDuff remarked, "changing plans at the last min."

"Nah, but I think it's fine."

"And we've got Paddy this time."

Hanson nodded. He and McDuff had been assigned to Lieutenant Mayne's party. "Man's a lunatic," he observed.

"The right kind of lunatic, Pete. And always better

to have those types on your side."

"True enough."

Their reduced convoy set off into the dry embrace of the new day, heading towards Tamet and their new target, targets they knew intimately, by sight and by outline, having spent hours months studying the enemy Stuka-J87s, Messerschmidt 109s and 110s, Caproni bombers. McDuff felt he could probably fly one of them so often had he read about the planes. So much was about igniting the fuel load, so their placement had to be perfect in the darkness and to get it right, they had to know the planes in detail. And so as they crawled along the desert track, warily scanning the scrub for an ambush and the sky for the marauding eyes of the enemy planes, McDuff went over again in his mind what they were hoping to find, picturing the layout of the aircraft, but also thinking on the briefing that covered the airfields. As ever, the ideal raid was to slip onto the airfields in the dead unnoticed and return to the welcoming comfort of the desert darkness without the enemy ever being the wiser, only knowing they'd been targeted when the first aircraft exploded to light up the night. So, he thought again of their task, the enemy they may encounter, and he prayed he would get it right.

It was late evening when their guide announced that they were now only a couple of miles away from their target, and McDuff shivered, but not with cold this time. Countless hours of training, countless false dawns, the failed operation a few weeks – was it only that long ago? – had all come and gone. He and this new means of waging war were less than twenty four hours away. And whilst he felt trepidation, he also grinned fiercely in the darkness. It was time. The men set to making a temporary camp in a low gully, camouflaging the trucks and preparing the evening meal. The mood was quiet, tense, but inescapably charged.

The evening hours ticked by with agonising lethargy until Mayne bestirred himself and raised his large frame, standing before them hands on hips. He was a big man, with a flat, broad forehead and nose, under which a mirthless smile seemed to be permanently lodged. It was a look that spoke of a certain arrogance and disdain for others, disdain that he rarely felt obliged to hide, especially when referring to the regular British Army. Whether it disguised a genuine insecurity and inner turmoil, McDuff neither knew nor cared. What he did know was that this was a man who knew how to fight, and so he tensed as Mayne spoke.

"It's time. Final check, then we move. Ready?"

There was a growl from the darkness, and Mayne's faced creased a little further. "I should hope so. Now move."

McDuff and the others finished their final round of checks, on machine guns, detonating time pencils and the precious Lewes bombs; anything that had a mechanical component had to be lovingly caressed and looked over, lest the sand that blighted them, found a way to make their fallible human technology fail them in their hour of need. But all was ready, and they trudged out into the dark behind Mayne and towards the enemy, moving steadily and carefully. It was a clear night and the temperature had dipped but the sweat still trickled down McDuff's back. They all carried rucksacks filled with their equipment, with faces blackened and an assortment of machine guns and rifles unslung and ready. They numbered ten men and, cautiously, they inched forward as they neared the airfield. McDuff's could hear the ragged breathing of Hanson behind him, sure he was the same and he suddenly wondered if he was breathing too loudly. The night was utterly still, a breath of air gently caressing them. It was in vivid contrast to their last effort, parachuting into a storm. Now conditions were set fair. He glanced into the sky and, even then his heart missed a beat as he took in the great blanket of stars that stretched from one horizon to the other. The stars and the desert had been there for aeons and would be there well after they had gone, and as ever, his awe was mingled with melancholy, which he shook off with an effort, refocusing on the task in hand.

Ahead of them, Mayne raised a hand and sank to one knee. "McDuff," he whispered. "With me."

McDuff scurried to the head of the column and knelt beside Mayne. They had come to rest at the bottom of a shallow gulley. "Over that ridge is the airfield," Mayne said. "Let's go take a look."

"Right you are, sir."

They scrambled up the shallow rise, sinking into the still warm sand. Something was startled out of its burrow and scurried away from them, a shrub rustling in the dark. Otherwise, the night was utterly still. Sand deadened any noise they made as they scrambled up. Nearing the top, Mayne held out a hand and they sank to their bellies, dragging themselves over the top. And there, lying before them, was their prize.

The airfield at Tamet was spread out and lay invitingly in front of them. McDuff slowly scanned the ground. Nothing seemed to stir in the faint moonlight. He noted the wire perimeter fence that wound its way around the airfield. Directly in front of him, the main event – the runway and the aircraft hangars. They lay parallel to the runway, which was bordered by several distance markers and a windsock that hung limply in the still night. Anti-aircraft emplacements were dotted around the edge. Turning his head to the left, several hangars were spread out around the edge of the airfield. They were open to the air, and he could see the wings of one aircraft peeping out, but the majority of the aircraft were parked up in neat rows. McDuff's heart beat hard at the sight of them, with something akin to longing. These were their targets that they'd spent so long working towards, studying and thinking about. The planes included the bold outlines of Italian Messerschmitt fighters and Stuka dive bombers. The control tower was unmistakable, a darker shape rising higher into the night sky, a viewing balcony winding its way round its circumference.

McDuff felt his arm seized in a firm grip and a fierce Irish burr in his ear. "Look at that McDuff, lots of targets."

McDuff grinned. "All just waiting for us."

Mayne pointed to their right, where there were a number of low, flat buildings. Above the doorway of several, shaded lamps threw a small circle of light. "Barracks." His finger settled on the largest building, and on the side a small rectangle of light peeked out from the hastily erected black out curtain. "Mess most likely."

At the far end of the airfield and distanced from the rest, two squat buildings lay darkened and menacing. McDuff gestured toward them. "Ammunition dumps?" he said. "Isolated for fire risk."

"Agreed. And petrol bowsers parked behind, can you see?"

McDuff moved slightly and made out the easily recognisable cylindrical shapes. "Yes, got them."

"Good. We'll take them with the aircraft." As they turned to leave, Mayne gripped McDuff's arm again. "Look," he said, and pointed.

It took McDuff a moment, but then he saw a faint glow in the gloom. His gut clenched. It was a sentry, and a careless one at that – he was smoking, cupping his cigarette but not enough to keep his location secret. Very slowly he was walking the perimeter of the airfield.

"We'll have to take him," Mayne breathed in his ear. "Quietly."

"Yes."

"Your man, Sergeant." Mayne was staring at him, as if assessing whether McDuff was up to the task.

McDuff stared back. This was what it had all been building to, the failed raids, the training, the boredom, the excitement. In this moment, he would find out if he was a soldier, and not just any soldier, but a raider from an elite force. He felt the fear, but underneath it a beating yearning to do this and do it well. "Yes, sir."

"Good. We'll brief the men and then head back. You first, take the sentry and we'll follow. Clear?"

"Crystal." They slithered back down the ridge to where the rest of the men were waiting. Mayne gathered them round and played back what they had seen. There were a few questions, but McDuff wasn't really listening. He was thinking about the Italian solider who was currently walking on his usual route around the airfield. The man was hundreds of miles behind the line, sleepy and bored. He may well have seen something about a small enemy patrol being spotted yesterday not far away, but by now he'd forgotten or discarded the information. He was thinking of home, of the food his mother used to make and the girl from next door he wanted to kiss. He was blissfully unaware that less than a mile away, a twenty year old farmer's son was currently thinking about the moment his knife would reach out to snuff out his life, of the right angle to make sure the man didn't shout and alert his comrades. The sentry was unaware of all of this and unaware that he was about to become the first official victim of the Special Air Service. He just kept walking while McDuff looked up to see Mayne looking at him with that curious smile. "Time to go, Sergeant." It was time

7

McDuff lay flat, eyes fixed on the sentry. A rock bit into his thigh but he ignored the sharp pain. They were striking in the early hours of the night, a time when men slept, and spirits sapped to their lowest ebb. It was the right time for the particular kind of killing the SAS were there to deliver - sudden, shocking and brutal.

McDuff had watched the man do his route twice, back and forth along the perimeter fence, so he could gauge the right moment to strike. The fence was the first obstacle. In the darkness, he slid forward until it took shape in front of his nose. His breath misted before him as he paused, listening, before taking out the bolt cutters that had been modified for ease of carry. Gritting his teeth, he placed the jaws around one of the threads near the bottom of the fence. He squeezed the cutters together as they bit down on the fence, gradually bringing more and more pressure to bear. Sweat trickled down his face. Finally, with a loud snap, the strand of the fence parted. McDuff waited anxiously, heart racing, waiting to see if the sentry had heard anything. But all remained still. He offered up a silent thank you. Moving the cutters, he attacked the next strand, working so the fence could be lifted to allow a man to slither through, but also easy enough to miss by a casual observer walking by.

Working quickly, he soon had enough room to wriggle through on his back, and he did so carefully. Behind him, he sensed the rest of the raiding party, although the sand deadened their soft scuffling. In front him, the airfield remained placid and still. It felt faintly unreal. Surely someone would notice them and shout? They'd seen several fixed emplacements that could only be machine gun nests, and he swallowed at the prospect of being caught out in the open. Stealth was their friend and so, inch by inch, he quietly worked his way towards the small cluster of rocks he'd scouted earlier. They lay just beyond the sentry's route and McDuff was hoping they would provide enough cover for him to close and kill the man. He knew the rest of the raiding party would be waiting, hidden, for him to do his work.

And so he waited. Waited for the sentry to turn on his heel at the end of his familiar route; to hitch his rifle a little more securely over his shoulder and begin to trudge back. By now the man was tired, bored and hungry. His shift stretched on and nothing was stirring in the darkness that he could see. It was the same route he had trudged a hundred times before. It was a safe posting, far behind the front line, offering an occasional distraction in the local town, but otherwise a welcome boredom. If he had happened to glance up, all he would have seen was the outline of the sand and the dunes stretching away seemingly infinitely into the darkness. He may have looked up at the sky, much as McDuff had, and wonder at the beauty that lay parallel to such savagery below. But most of all, he thought of when his shift would end, of how good his breakfast would taste and how nice it would be to lay his head down on his pillow.

McDuff's nose crinkled as the man passed. In the crisp desert air, the scent of smoke and unwashed clothes was sharp and vivid to his enlivened senses. A few small stones were scattered by the sentry's boots, letting McDuff gauge the exact moment at which to rise silently, drawing his knife smoothly out, moving rapidly forward. His eyes, wide and staring, fixed on the back of the sentry's head, noting the coarse dark hair that spilled out under the forage cap, and the glint of a silver chain that he momentarily thought could be a crucifix. If it was, the sentry's God had deserted him that night. McDuff thrust the thought aside, his heartbeat throbbing in his head, an unstoppable torrent of adrenalin moving him forward, and he realised he was holding his breath and only exhaled explosively as he struck.

Wrapping his left hand around the sentry's face, he yanked it back, feeling the stubble scraping over his palm as he tried to smother the sentry's mouth, desperate to prevent any noise escaping. In his other hand, the knife was suddenly in front of them both, a faint glint in the moonlight. The sentry, who had been momentarily frozen, bucked and twisted wildly at the sight, a strange keening rising from within him, but it was too late. The blade flashed across his throat and McDuff sensed the warm spurt of sticky fluid that spattered wetly onto the sand around them. A faintly metallic scent rose to join that of sweat and fear. The sentry buckled, falling to his knees, his hands scrabbling at his throat, even as he tried to turn his head to see the demon that had appeared out of the darkness to snatch his life away. McDuff edged back, instinctively shying away from seeing the sentry's face in his final throes. A muscle twitched in his upper arm as he watched, and when, finally, the sentry toppled forward, a ball of nausea and fierce exhilaration simultaneously flowed through him.

For a long moment, he stared down at the body, absentmindedly wiping the sweat that dripped off his face. The knife hung by his side, a viscous snake of blood inching down the blade to drip onto the sand. So intent was his concentration, he didn't hear the approach of the other members of the raiding party until a hand rested on his shoulder.

"Christ," he said involuntarily, jumping at the touch.

"Calm down, McDuff." Mayne's amused Irish burr was at McDuff's ear. "That was a bit lively wasn't it?"

"Something like that." McDuff grinned as exultation began to replace his fear. "Messy."

"It usually is, McDuff, it usually is. Now come on."

Silently, they ghosted forward onto the airfield. Each man carried a simple haversack that contained the precious Lewes bombs, as well as their personal small arms. The only sounds were the soft scuffing of their boots on the runway, covered in a fine sheen of sand and the panting of men hyped up with fear and excitement. McDuff's eyes darted wildly around, finding the machine gun nests on the corner of the airfield. They remained mercifully still. A few hundred yards away the small cluster of buildings stood. A small light peeked out from under the poorly blacked out window. McDuff gave it a wary look and then turned back as they came upon the first of the enemy aircraft.

There were dozens of them, all parked invitingly in neat rows. In the dim light, McDuff could make out the sleek outline of the famous Messerschmidt 109, a predator of the daytime sky and an elegant killer of

Allied aircraft and crew. He grinned, almost doing a jig on the spot, sucking the crisp desert air into his lungs. "We've caught them with their pants down!" he whispered to Hanson, who gave a thumbs up back, his white teeth flashing. McDuff ran his hand over the next aircraft, realising that the outline had changed. It was a Stuka! The Junkers 87, hyena of the sky, that hunted in a pack with pinpoint accuracy, was a valuable kill. He could scarcely contain himself and began to open the haversack, but Mayne appeared in front of them

"Not yet," he said.

McDuff stared at him. "Not yet?"

"We've got business over there first." Mayne gestured with his head to the huts. "McDuff, Hanson, Seekings, with me."

"What about the planes?"

"We'll do them after."

"Is that – "

"Cut your noise, Sergeant," Mayne growled. "Let's go."

Mayne moved off and Hanson looked at McDuff. "Crazy Mick."

"Isn't he just," McDuff murmured. They were ignoring operational protocol if they were attacking the enemy personnel directly. It was secondary to their target and would simply alert the enemy to their presence. They were hunters, stalking their prey and making the kill through guile as much as guts, trained to avoid the enemy where possible. This diversion not only went against that training but made the whole mission more dangerous. It was reckless when the operation was going according to plan. Yet part of McDuff thrilled to the idea, of tweaking the tail of the tiger in its own back yard. Damn the rules, damn the enemy and let them come to fear the name of the SAS. He turned to Hanson. "In for a penny, in for a pound," he said clapping Hanson on the shoulder before hurrying after Mayne.

Cautiously, they approached the hut, flattening themselves either side of the door. They paused. From within came the sound of raised voices, the clink of glasses and a German folk tune.

"Dreadful noise," Mayne said, as he checked his revolver, a Colt. 45 that would kill a man dead in such a confined space.

McDuff smiled mirthlessly as he checked his Thompson machine gun, regulating his breathing. "Must be something to celebrate."

"Won't be celebrating in a minute," Hanson said grimly.

"Ready?"

"Ready."

Mayne moved to stand in front of the door. McDuff gazed at him in the split second before he moved, outlined in the faint light. His uniform, tatty and dirty as they all were, hung on his body. His ragged beard framed the hard lines of his face with its prominent nose, and the faintest hint of a smirk caught the edge of his mouth. In this right hand the revolver nestled, like a toy gun in the giant paw of the wild Irishman. His other hand was balled into a fist. A slight movement of his chest revealed the breath he took, before he raised the scuffed, vast boot and bought it crashing into the door.

The door rocked back against its hinges before bouncing back towards Mayne, who was already moving forward, McDuff at his heels. Pushing back the door, they strode into the hut, Hanson and Seekings with them. They were in a pilot's mess. A fug of tobacco smoke hung over the room, stirred by a lazily turning fan. McDuff could see several tables laid out, their long benches dotted with young men who stared in amazement at the raiders, frozen in a series of vignettes of mess life – several were playing cards, others having a final bite of supper or simply enjoying a drink and a song. One corner of the room contained a battered sofa and several comfortable looking armchairs. An officer sat in one of them, the small dog in his lap raising its head at the sudden intrusion, ears pricked. Directly opposite them, a barman stood, paralysed in the act of polishing a glass, mouth slightly agape. Behind him, a sun faded picture of Hitler hung on the wall. On the other was a blackboard with a list of names and chalk markings – Muller, Scholz, Seehofer, Mass. It was a tally board, McDuff realised, listing the number of kills each pilot had made. Underneath it was a cartoonish eagle, evidently the unit's unofficial insignia. Both sides looked at each and all the time the tenor warbled away on the record player, a jaunty sound at odds with the sudden chill of incomprehension and fear that had come over the room.

The spell was broken when a German officer near the door spoke. "Italiano?" he asked tentatively.

"Inglese," Mayne replied and shot him, the man's head snapping back, a mist of blood splattering the men nearest to him. The discharge was shockingly loud in the confined space, and it was the signal for pandemonium. McDuff and Hanson began firing their machine guns into the mass of pilots, who were now shouting and screaming in fear and anger as they dived onto the floor, trying to find any scrap of cover. The magazine in McDuff's Thompson clicked just as he swept it through the sitting area in the corner, and a small part of his mind noted in relief that the weapon stopped before his fire reached the dog. The pilots were desperately scrabbling for their sidearms and other weapons. One man tried to lever open the window, but Hanson saw him, jerking his machine gun up and cutting the man down. He slumped to the ground, just as more men jostled to try and escape from the windows. Hanson cursed as he reloaded.

"Grenades!" shouted Mayne, and several were launched to where some of the pilots had gone to ground. But some of the pilots began to return fire, ducking out of cover to snipe at the raiders who were dangerously exposed in the open doorway. McDuff flinched as bullets struck the wall around him, a wooden splinter ricocheting past him. He fumbled another magazine, risking a glance at Mayne, who was lining up his revolver and firing methodically, arm outstretched. As the hammer clicked on an empty chamber, he turned to the McDuff. "That's enough, back!"

McDuff barrelled out of the door, but as he did so, a figure burst out of the night and crashed into him, sending them both against the wall of the hut. The man cursed in German as they grappled. Hanson tried to bring the butt of his gun down on the German's head, but the man was solidly built and twisted wildly, and the blow glanced off the German and into McDuff's shoulder. McDuff strained to bring his weapon to bear but it was trapped in between them, the barrel poking useless to one side. The German was using his heavier bulk to pin McDuff against the wall while trying to knee McDuff in the groin. The smell of the man's breath, a fetid mix of garlic and beer, wafted over McDuff, as nausea and anger raged through him. The German's arms were solid and slippery with sweat and he couldn't get purchase to lever the man away. Moving his head back slightly, he bought his hard down into the German's face, feeling a blinding lance of pain but the man's bear hug loosened immediately, and McDuff managed to thrust him away. The German staggered back a few steps and Hanson, standing to one side, stepped forward and shot him.

"Thanks," McDuff said, panting.

"Pleasure."

"Where the hell did he come from?"

"No idea, but they know we're here now, and there's probably more of the bastards on the way."

"If you're finished catching up," Mayne intervened. "Let's go."

They melted back into the darkness and ghosted to where the rest of the raiding party waited. "Seekings, Gilchrest, Hislop, Cooper. Stay here and cover the huts. We can expect some company shortly. Anything that comes this way, shoot it. Clear?"

"Clear."

"We're going to get the planes, then pull back. The rest of you – Hunt, Wallace, Hannagan with me and the planes. McDuff, Hanson, petrol bowsers and ammo dump."

The man fanned out and began placing the bombs on the aircraft as they appeared out of the darkness. Each time, they had to make sure which aircraft they were targeting - the bombs had to be placed as close to the fuel tank as possible. It was the high-octane aviation fuel in the tanks that was needed to ensure a proper bonfire of the aircraft. Each aircraft was checked over and a suitable spot found for the bomb. In the Me 109 fighter, the fuel tank was largely under and behind the cockpit, while the JU87 dive-bomber had the main tank to one side of the cockpit on the wing. Each of the raiding party had spent hours examining and learning the details of both German and Italian aircraft and now that training paid off. In the darkness, hands slippery with sweat and hearts pounding, they forced themselves to work methodically, ignoring the sounds of gunfire that still punctuated the air from the direction of the mess hut.

McDuff glanced back as he and Hanson sprinted towards the far end of the airfield. Tracer fire spat out of the darkness, adding a ghoulish green hue to the battle. It was answered by the flashes of the blocking force, who had placed bombs on the nearest huts and pulled back into the dark. They kept a sporadic fire on any enemy that appeared, who were still reeling from the onslaught. McDuff grinned. The SAS had appeared like wolves from the night to tear into the unsuspecting enemy, an enemy who were demoralised and feeling pain. Now was the time to add to the chaos.

As he turned to Hanson, the hyena chatter of a heavy machine gun ripped through the night, spitting venom. The angry zip of flying metal flashed terrifyingly close to McDuff and Hanson, and they threw themselves to the ground. They were still a hundred yards from their targets and exposed on the black tarmac.

"Where the hell did that come from?" Hanson shouted as they frantically shunted forward on their bellies.

"They've woken up! It's those bloody gun

emplacements!"

"Can we make it?"

McDuff risked a glance back. They would be hard to pick out in the darkness, and that could give them a chance. Yet even as he had the thought, a violent hissing noise erupted as a flare rocketed into the night sky, casting a harsh glare over the airfield.

"No choice! Come on!"

Pushing themselves upright, they sprinted towards the far end of the airfield, zig zagging desperately. Sparks showed up on the tarmac as bullets ricocheted around them. McDuff's blood was pounding through his body, his breath coming in aching gasps as he pumped his legs, desperately seeking the shelter among the small cluster of buildings that came rapidly into view. He felt like a deer in the headlights of a car, and almost shouted in relief as they reached a small barrier, waist high, which bordered the runway. Without breaking stride, he and Hanson hurled themselves over it, rolling in the dust to come to a halt on their backs, panting heavily.

For a moment, McDuff watched his breath fogging in front of him, blinking the sweat from his eyes. Bullets smacked into the barrier and he turned his head to look at Hanson, who seemed to be mouthing the same words over and over.

"What are you saying?"

"Don't ever volunteer for anything ever again."

McDuff laughed and reached out his hand, pulling Hanson up with him. They crept to the barrier, peeking over, but no gun fire answered them, and he frowned. What were they playing at? Then the machine gun opened up again and he cursed. The gunners daren't fire on the raiders among the planes but if the Germans could kill off the blocking force, they could overrun the raiders. And even if they didn't, the machine gun was now directly in the path of their escape route back into the desert.

"We've got to get that gun," he said grimly, reloading the Thompson.

"Agreed. Let's get the bombs on these first."

McDuff hesitated, but only for a moment. Precious seconds would be lost, but the mission was first. "Come on, hurry."

Rapidly, they began affixing multiple bombs to the petrol bower and the ammunition dump. A smaller hut, standing slightly away from the others, had a skull and cross bones affixed to the door. He couldn't decipher the German, but he figured whatever was in there was going to be very nasty if blown up. Tenderly, he placed several bombs around the hut and then hurried back towards the Hanson, his steps given impetus by the renewed outbreak of firing coming from the airfield. The duller crump of detonating grenades mixed with the sharper report of rifle and the frenzied natter of the machine gun in a discordant orchestra that lent a surreal aspect to the beautiful desert night.

As he neared the barrier, he glimpsed something partially hidden behind the ammunition dump. It took a moment, but he realised that poking out from under a tarpaulin was a wheel. Seeing that Gilcrest was still scurrying round the other huts placing bombs, he jogged over and pulled back the tarpaulin. Underneath was an open topped Küblewagen, the ubiquitous German army jeep. It had no doors and he slid into the bucket seat, an idea forming in his mind. Swiftly he scanned the controls and, with a leap, saw the key hanging in the ignition. Turning the key, the engine roared into life and he grinned. He leant back and carefully reversed out, driving over to Hanson who had appeared.

"What are we doing, Jim?"

"Get in the driver's seat. We're going to get that gun."

Realisation dawned and Hanson gave a thumbs up, sliding into the driver's seat while McDuff hopped into the back and stood ready. He reloaded the Thompson and gripped the roll bar before looking down at Hanson.

"Ready?"

"As I'll ever be."

"Let's go."

Hanson nosed out in a gap in the barrier onto the airfield proper, before gunning the engine and heading directly towards the sound of gunfire. Their speed picked up rapidly and McDuff had to shout down to Hanson to ease off as he bucked and swayed in the back. Settling down into a steady pace, McDuff scanned the battle which was raging before them. The raiders were spread out, firing swift bursts before rushing back but their progress was hampered by the machine gunner. With only ten men, they were in danger of being overwhelmed. As they drove on, one of the bombs on the huts detonated, and flames eagerly began to spill out. Several German and Italian soldiers and pilots scrambled to get clear, their hunched bodies silhouetted against the flames as they fell back. One threw up his hands and collapsed as he ran, but McDuff could also glimpse more enemy troops creeping closer, working their way forward. Their fear of hurting their own planes was forcing them to be cautious but their plan was clear.

"They're going to keep them pinned down with the gun and flank them!" McDuff shouted.

Hanson nodded in assent and switched gears, the engine roaring, as they shot forward. They bumped over the ground, the cold air buffeting McDuff in the back. He prayed. Prayed the gunners would keep their focus on the rest of the raiding party; prayed they wouldn't look round. And prayed that his aim would stay true as he launched their attack.

They were closing fast when a cry sounded from the gun emplacement. Shaped in a protective horseshoe, it was made up of sandbags and crates. A camouflage awning offered protection from sun and enemy plane alike. Underneath, McDuff could see the outline of shapes as the gunners went about their work. There were two gaps at either end where the machine gun could be moved to dominate the airfield in front of them and now the men were frenziedly moving the gun so that it could be bough to bear on their Kübelwagen and McDuff felt his fear rising.

"Faster!" he shouted, desperate to close into effective range before the gun could begin. He braced himself and lifted the Thompson as they draw closer, trying to line up on the gunners. Taking a deep breath, he squeezed the trigger, watching as puffs of dirt began flying up from around the emplacement. Sandbags were holed, their contents spilling out, and McDuff kept the trigger held down as they swept by, feeling the recoil but seeing, too, that his wild spray of fire had found its mark. One gunner was flung back, holding his shoulder but his comrade managed to squeeze off a burst that raked the Kübelwagen, shattering the windscreen and stitching a line of bullet holes across the side that ended in the rear wheel, which burst with the sound of a gunshot.

Immediately, the Kübelwagen swerved violently, Hanson cursing wildly as he fought to maintain control, desperately sawing at the wheel and feathering the brake. But he was fighting a losing battle, and the momentum coupled with the sudden change in direction could only end one way. The jeep bucked and then began to tilt. McDuff was already over balancing and threw himself to one side, grateful for the training Lieutenant Lewes had put together for them. He gasped as the wind was driven out of him, pain lancing through his shoulder as he sprawled across the floor. Lifting himself up on his elbow he saw the Kübelwagen on its side and breathed a sigh of relief as he glimpsed Hanson crawling out from the driver's side, a trickle of blood snaking down his face.

Another burst of fire from the machine gun slammed into the jeep, a small fire breaking out above the engine block. Hanson cowered as the gun raked the jeep again. McDuff looked round. Rifle fire spat out of the darkness toward him as he rose, grimacing in discomfort. Keeping low, he trusted that he was hidden enough from the bulk of the enemy force. He looked at the machine gun emplacement. It seemed that the gunner hadn't seen him come to rest and he was out to one side, out of the field of fire. He quickly covered the short distance to the gun, fumbling for a grenade. The fire from the jeep and the huts cast a muffled glow around him and he glimpsed the final gunner cocking the machine gun in the pit. The gunner was intent on the jeep and the men in front of him and McDuff closed, taking the grenade and lobbing it deftly over the sandbags. He collapsed and planted his face in the dirt. Moments later a dull thud reverberated, and the camouflage net billowed out, dirt and wicked shards of metal flying outward. Cautiously raising his head, McDuff saw the gunner flung forward over the sandbags, wisps of smoke coming from his charred uniform.

Around him, the raiders turned their fire onto the remaining force and with the machine gun silenced their way back into the desert expanse was clear. McDuff hurried over to the wreck, where he found Hanson, who was grimacing in pain.

"Knew you couldn't drive."

"Knew you couldn't shoot straight."

Gripping Hanson by the shoulders, McDuff heaved him upright and began to limp toward the rest of the party.

"Give them cover!" Mayne's voice sounded clearly out of the darkness. "And give Hanson a hand. Seekings, Cooper – you are rearguard. Keep those bastard's heads down. And don't get lost, we won't wait."

"Am I glad to see you, sir," McDuff panted.

"Good work, Sergeant. Hanson, how bad is it?"

"I can make it, it's just sore."

"Good. Because if you can't walk, we have to leave you."

The raiders hurried back across the airfield, intermittent fire pursuing them. As they neared the end, they passed several Italian Caproni bombers parked up.

"Anyone got any more bombs?" Mayne asked.

The raiders indicated they were out. "Fine. Give them a volley and then we'll go."

Swiftly, the men fanned out, clambering up onto the

planes. Changing his magazine, McDuff took aim at the control panels and emptied his Thompson into it. Around him the other raiders did the same, and McDuff jumped down, grinning.

"That should clip their wings."

They jogged on until they reached the perimeter fence at the edge of the airfield. Dispensing with stealth, they ripped it apart swiftly and headed out into the open desert. Hanson was limping but gritting his teeth and keeping up. There was a tangible sense of excitement and exhilaration amongst the group, which was only heightened moments later.

They'd scarcely gone a hundred yards before the first bomb went off. As one, the raiding party turned and looked back. A finger of fire and black smoke billowed into the sky. One by one the other bombs began exploding, flames rising to the sky, but the final note was about to come. With a deafening roar, the petrol and ammunition dumps went up. A great mushroom of fire lit the sky, interspaced with the flashes from the bombs going off on the remaining planes. A cheer went up from the group. In the face of a hostile bureaucracy, an implacable desert and the enemy, they'd pulled off something many had felt was impossible. They'd bearded the enemy in their den and, in doing so, had secured the future of the Special Air Service. Ten men had destroyed dozens of planes and killed many pilots, all without taking a single casualty. No one could touch them. McDuff hugged Hanson.

"We did it."

HISTORICAL NOTE

Always a Little Further is based on the real history of the founding of the Special Air Service and the themes it explores are entirely true. It was, at the outset, never a unit that was wanted by large parts of the British High Command. They felt it contravened the norms of war as well as the chain of command. To many, it simply 'not British' to be striking far behind the enemy lines, instead of in pitched and conventional battle. Thankfully, that view did not prevail, but it is was a close run thing and it is striking that the unit was born in a theatre of war noted for the 'chivalry' in which it was conducted. This had much to do with the environment it was fought in – the desert, the common enemy, as was famously said at the end of the classic war film, Ice Cold in Alex, was a deadly enemy to all sides, and earned their respect and fear. However, it was the British, rather than the Axis forces, who really learnt to exploit it with special forces. Although the various forces that made up the irregular side of the Western Desert Force were a truly multinational effort, reflecting how much of a world war it was. New Zealanders were particularly well represented amongst the Long Range Desert Group (LRDG) and the SAS would go on to have a specific French and Belgian units later in the war, as well as members of countless other nationalities.

The LRDG are arguably underrepresented in the public consciousness when it comes to the story of the SAS. Without them, the SAS would not have been as successful, as the calamitous first parachute raid covered at the start of this novella shows. They were the real masters of the desert when the SAS were founded, operating as the eyes and ears of the British Army and their role in helping the SAS grow was critical. Much like the SAS, they were founded and led by another unorthodox genius, Major Ralph Bagnold, explorer, scientists, archaeologist and world authority on sand. He had been the first to successfully drive across the Libyan desert, a journey of over 3,000 miles and his contributions to how to work with the desert – from his sun compass, to tyre pressures and many others – were incalculably important. In mid 1940 he was given permission to form a mobile scouting force, and thus the Long Range Patrol (later the LRDG) was born.

Captain David Stirling was an equally unorthodox and brilliant man. Indeed, the history of special forces is littered with them. He came from an old military family but spent most of his time at university gambling and carousing. A civilian life lacking in distinction incorporated being an artist, an architect, and a mountaineer. He was successful at none but had a flair for war. However, his previous habits were not constrained by army life at first. When it bored him, which it did frequently, he ignored his responsibilities and often went drinking. Nonetheless, he had a keen mind and a thirst for adventure, which led him naturally to special forces. And it was his personality – dismissive of hierarchy and objection, completely confident in his view – that led to the setting up of the SAS (as well as a personal connection to General Claude Auchinleck). He was a unique individual and made a huge contribution to the war.

The story of the first disastrous raid is entirely true. The weather was atrocious, and arguably the SAS should never have been deployed, but that wouldn't have stopped Stirling or the others – Lewes and Mayne – particularly when they were keenly aware (and eager) to prove themselves. The ensuing operation could have killed the idea of the SAS stone dead, but among the maelstrom of Rommel's counter stroke and more pressing issues, giving the SAS another chance was a shot to nothing. If it went wrong, a few men would be lost; if it went well, it could be of benefit. No one thought it would be quite so effective as it was, however, and when the SAS went back to the same airfields only weeks after the first successful raids, the shot to nothing had paid the most handsome of dividends.

For anyone wishing to read a comprehensive and enjoyable account of these early days, I'd recommend Ben Macintyre's SAS: Rouge Heroes – The Authorised Wartime History, from which much of my novella is derived. It provides a fascinating insight into the early days and the list of characters who populated the unit then, as well as the full history of the Regiment.

The desert was where the SAS was born and where many of the 'Originals' would lay forever. However, after this first spectacular success, Sergeant McDuff and his fellow rogues have plenty more battles to fight, moving from the desert into mainland Europe and some of the most consequential battles of the war. They will march again, always a little further, and you can keep up to date on their progress at www.timothyoliver.co.uk. My thanks for reading. I hope you enjoyed it and if so, please feel free to leave a review on Amazon saying so!

Tim Oliver, June 2020

Printed in Great Britain
by Amazon

49839997R00066